NOCTURNA

of dust through which the flying animals were dimly visible like phantom figures. Kublai Khan was choked, and his hot breath rasped sharply through his nostrils, but he plunged on and on into that yellow cloud. Standing in my stirrups, I fired six times at the wraithlike forms ahead as fast as I could work the lever of my rifle. Of course, it was useless, but just the same I had to shoot.

In about a mile the great herd slowed down and stopped. We could see hundreds of animals on every side, in groups of fifty or one hundred. Probably two thousand antelope were in sight at once and many more were beyond the sky rim to the west. We gave the ponies ten minutes' rest, and had another run as unsuccessful as the first. Then a third and fourth. The antelope, for some strange reason, would not cross our path, but always turned straight away before we were near enough to shoot.

After an hour we returned to the carts—for Yvette was exhausted from excitement—and the lama took her place. We left the great herd and turned southward, parallel to the road. A mile away we found more antelope; at least a thousand were scattered about feeding quietly like those we had driven north. It seemed as though all the gazelles in Mongolia had concentrated on those few miles of plain.

The ponies were so exhausted that we decided to try a drive and leave the main herd in peace. When we were concealed from view in the bottom of a land swell I slipped off and hobbled Kublai Khan. The poor fellow was so tired he could only stand with drooping head, even though there was rich grass beneath his feet. I sent the lama in a long circle to get behind the herd, while I crawled a few hundred yards away and snuggled out of sight into an old wolf den.

I watched the antelope for fifteen minutes through my binoculars. They were feeding in a vast semicircle, entirely unconscious of my presence. Suddenly every head went up; they stared fixedly toward the west for a moment, and were off like the wind. About five hundred drew together in a compact mass, but a dozen smaller herds scattered wildly, running in every direction except toward me. They had seen the lama before he had succeeded in completely encircling them, and the drive was ruined.

The Mongols kill great numbers of antelope in just this way. When a herd has been located, a line of men will conceal themselves at distances of two or three hundred yards, while as many more get behind the animals and drive them toward the waiting hunters. Sometimes the gazelles almost step on the natives and become so frightened that they run the gantlet of the entire firing line.

I did not have the heart to race again with our exhausted ponies, and we turned back toward the carts which were out of sight. Scores of antelope, singly or in pairs, were visible on the sky line and as we rode to the summit of a little rise a herd of fifty appeared almost below us. We paid no attention to them; but suddenly my pony stopped with ears erect. He looked back at me, as much as to say, "Don't you see those antelope?" and began gently pulling at the reins. I could feel him tremble with eagerness and excitement. "Well, old chap," I said, "if you are as keen as all that, let's give them a run."

With a magnificent burst of speed Kublai Khan launched himself toward the fleeing animals. They circled beautifully, straight into the eye of the sun, which lay like a great red ball upon the surface of the plain. We were still three hundred yards away and gaining rapidly, but I had to shoot; in a moment I would be blinded by the sun. As the flame leaped from my rifle, we heard the dull thud of a bullet on flesh; at the second shot, another; and then a third. "*Sanga*" (three), yelled the lama, and dashed forward, wild with excitement.

The three gazelles lay almost the same distance apart, each one shot through the body. It was interesting evidence that the actions of working the lever on my rifle and aiming, and the speed of the antelope, varied only by a fraction of a second. In this case, brain and eye and hand had functioned perfectly. Needless to say, I do not always shoot like that.

Two of the antelope were yearling bucks, and one was a large doe. The lama took the female on his pony, and I strapped the other two on Kublai Khan. When I mounted, he was carrying a weight of two hundred and eighty-five pounds, yet he kept his steady "homeward trot" without a break until we reached the carts six miles away.

Yvette had been afraid that we would miss the well in the

gathering darkness, and had made a "dry camp" beside the road. We had only a little water for ourselves; but my pony's nose was full of dust, and I knew how parched his throat must be, so I divided my supply with him. The poor animal was so frightened by the dish, that he would only snort and back away; even when I wet his nose with some of the precious fluid, he would not drink.

The success of our work upon the plains depended largely upon Kublai Khan. He was only a Mongol pony but he was just as great, in his own way, as was the Tartar emperor whose name he bore. Whatever it was I asked him to do, he gave his very best. Can you wonder that I loved him?

Within a fortnight from the time I bought him, he became a perfect hunting pony. The secret of it all was that he liked the game as well as I. Traveling with the carts bored him exceedingly but the instant game appeared he was all excitement. Often he saw antelope before we did. We might be trotting slowly over the plains, when suddenly he would jerk his head erect and begin to pull gently at the reins; when I reached down to take my rifle from the holster, he would tremble with eagerness to be off.

In hunting antelope you should ride slowly toward the animals, drawing nearer gradually. They are so accustomed to see Mongols that they will not begin to run in earnest until a man is five or six hundred yards away, but when they are really off, a fast pony is the great essential. The time to stop is just before the animals cross your path, and then you must stop quickly. Kublai Khan learned the trick immediately. As soon as he felt the pressure of my knees, and the slightest pull upon the reins, his whole body stiffened and he braced himself like a polo pony. It made not the slightest difference to him whether I shot from his back or directly under his nose; he stood quietly watching the running antelope. When we were riding across the plaints if a bird ran along the ground or a hare jumped out of the grass, he was after it like a dog. Often I would find myself flying toward an animal which I had never seen.

Yvette's pony was useless for hunting antelope. Instead of heading diagonally toward the gazelles he would always attempt to follow the herd. When it was time to stop I would have to put all my strength upon the reins and the horse would come into a slow gallop and then a trot. Seconds of valuable time would be wasted before I could begin to shoot. I tried half a dozen other ponies, but they were all as bad. They did not have the intelligence or the love of hunting which made Kublai Khan so valuable.

The morning after encountering the great herd, we camped at a well thirty miles north of the Turin monastery. Three or four *yurts* were scattered about, and a caravan of two hundred and fifty camels was resting in a little hollow. From the door of our tent we could see the blue summit of the Turin "mountain," and have in the foreground a perpetual moving picture of camels, horses, sheep, goats, and cattle seeking water. All day long hundreds of animals crowded about the well, while one or two Mongols filled the troughs by means of wooden buckets.

The life about the wells is always interesting, for they are points of concentration for all wanderers on the plains. Just as we pitch our tents and make ourselves at home, so great caravans arrive with tired, laden camels. The huge brutes kneel, while their packs are being removed, and then stand in a long line, patiently waiting until their turn comes to drink. Groups of ten or twelve crowd about the trough; then, majestically swinging their padded feet, they move slowly to one side, kneel upon the ground, and sleepily chew their cuds until all the herd has joined them. Sometimes the caravans wait for several days to rest their animals and let them feed; sometimes they vanish in the first gray light of dawn.

On the Turin plain we had a delightful glimpse of antelope babyhood. The great herds which we had found were largely composed of does just ready to drop their young, and after a few days they scattered widely into groups of from five to twenty.

We found the first baby antelope on June 27. We had seen half a dozen females circling restlessly about, and suspected that their fawns could not be far away. Sure enough, our Mongol discovered one of the little fellows in the flattest part of the flat plain. It was lying motionless with its neck stretched out, just where its mother had told it to remain when she saw us riding toward her.

Yvette called to me, "Oh, please, please catch it. We can raise it on milk and it will make such an adorable pet."

"Oh, yes," I said, "let's do. I'll get it for you. You can put it in your hat till we go back to camp."

In blissful ignorance I dismounted and slowly went toward the little animal. There was not the slightest motion until I tossed my outspread shooting coat. Then I saw a flash of brown, a bobbing white rump-patch, and a tiny thing, no larger than a rabbit, speeding over the plain. The baby was somewhat "wabbly," to be sure, for this was probably the first time it had ever tried its slender legs, but after a few hundred yards it ran as steadily as its mother.

I was so surprised that for a moment I simply stared. Then I leaped into the saddle and Kublai Khan rushed after the diminutive brown fawn. It was a good half mile before we had the little chap under the pony's nose but the race was by no means ended. Mewing with fright, it swerved sharply to the left and ere we could swing about, it had gained a hundred yards. Again and again we were almost on it, but every time it dodged and got away. After half an hour my pony was gasping for breath, and I changed to Yvette's chestnut stallion. The Mongol joined me and we had another run, but we might have been pursuing a streak of shifting sunlight. Finally we had to give it up and watch the tiny thing bob away toward its mother, who was circling about in the distance.

There were half a dozen other fawns upon the plain, but they all treated us alike and my wife's hat was empty when we returned to camp. These antelope probably had been born not more than two or three days before we found them. Later, after a chase of more than a mile, we caught one which was only a few hours old. Had it not injured itself when dodging between my pony's legs we could never have secured it at all.

Thus, nature, in the great scheme of life, has provided for her antelope children by blessing them with undreamed-of speed and only during the first days of babyhood could a wolf catch them on the open plain. When they are from two to three weeks old they run with the females in herds of six or eight, and you cannot imagine what a pretty sight it is to see the little fellows skimming like tiny, brown chickens beside their mothers. There is another wonderful provision for their life upon the desert. The digestive fluids of the stomach act upon the starch in the vegetation which they eat so that it forms sufficient water for their needs. Therefore, some species never drink.

The antelope choose a flat plain on which to give birth to their young in order to be well away from the wolves which are their greatest enemy; and the fawns are taught to lie absolutely motionless upon the ground until they know that they have been discovered. Apparently they are all born during the last days of June and in the first week of July. The great herds which we encountered were probably moving northward both to obtain better grazing and to drop their young on the Turin plain. During this period the old bucks go off singly into the rolling ground, and the herds are composed only of does and yearling males. It was always possible to tell at once if an antelope had a fawn upon the plain, for she would run in a wide circle around the spot and refuse to be driven away.

We encountered only two species of antelope between Kalgan and Urga. The one of which I have been writing, and with which we became best acquainted, was the Mongolian gazelle (*Gazella gutturosa*). The other was the goitered gazelle (*Gazella subgutturosa*). In the western Gobi, the Prjevalski gazelle (*Gazella prjevalski*) is more abundant than the other species, but it never reaches the region which we visited.

The goitered antelope is seldom found on the rolling meadowlands between Kalgan and Panj-kiang on the south, or between Turin and Urga on the north, according to our observations; they keep almost entirely to the Gobi Desert between Panj-kiang and Turin, and we often saw them among the "nigger heads" or tussocks in the most arid parts. The Mongolian gazelle, on the other hand, is most abundant in the grasslands both north and south of the Gobi, but nevertheless has a continuous distribution across the plateau between Kalgan and Urga.

On our northward trip in May, when we took motion pictures of the antelope on the Panj-kiang plain, both, species were present, but the goitered gazelle far outnumbered the others—which is unusual in that locality. It could always be distinguished from the Mongolian gazelle because of its smaller size, darker coloring, and the long tail which it carries straight up in the air at right angles to the back; the Mongolian antelope has an exceedingly short tail. The horns of both species differ considerably in shape and can easily be distinguished.

During the winter these antelope develop a coat of very long, soft hair which is light brown-gray in color strongly tinged with rufous on the head and face. Its summer pelage is a beautiful orange-fawn. The winter coat is shed during May, and the animals lose their short summer hair in late August and early September.

Both species have a greatly enlarged larynx from which the goitered gazelle derives its name. What purpose this extraordinary character serves the animal, I am at a loss to know. Certainly it is not to give them an exceptional "voice"; for, when wounded, I have heard them make only a deep-toned roar which was by no means loud. Specimens of the larynx which we preserved in formalin are now being prepared for anatomical study.

Although the two species inhabit the same locality, they keep well by themselves and only once, on the Panj-kiang plain, did we see them running together in the same herd; then it was probably because they were frightened by the car. I doubt if they ever interbreed except in rare instances.

The fact that these animals can develop such an extraordinary speed was a great surprise to me, as undoubtedly it will be to most naturalists. Had we not been able to determine it accurately by means of the speedometers on our cars, I should never have dared state that they could reach fifty-five or sixty miles an hour. It must be remembered that the animals can continue at such a high speed only for a short distance—perhaps half a mile—and will never exert themselves to the utmost unless they are thoroughly frightened. They would run just fast enough to keep well away from the cars or our horses, and it was only when we began to shoot that they showed what they were capable of doing. When the bullets began to scatter about them they would seem to flatten several inches and run at such a terrific speed that their legs appeared only as a blur.

Of course, they have developed their fleetness as a protection from enemies. Their greatest menace is the wolves, but since we demonstrated that these animals cannot travel faster than about thirty miles an hour, the antelope are perfectly safe unless they happen to be caught off their guard. To prevent just this, the gazelles usually keep well out on the open plains and avoid rocks or abrupt hills which would furnish cover for a wolf. Of course, they often go into the rolling ground, but it is usually where the slopes are gradual and where they have sufficient space in which to protect themselves.

The gazelles have a perfectly smooth, even run when going at full speed. I have often seen them bound along when not particularly frightened, but never when they are really trying to get away in the shortest possible time. The front limbs, as in the case of a deer, act largely as supports and the real motive power comes from the hind legs. If an antelope has only a front leg broken no living horse can catch it, but with a shattered hind limb my pony could run it down. I have already related how, in a car, we pursued an antelope with both front legs broken below the knee; even then, it reached a speed of fifteen miles an hour. The Mongolian plains are firm and hard with no bushes or other obstructions and, consequently, are especially favorable for rapid travel.

The cheetah, or hunting leopard of Africa, has the reputation of being able to reach a greater speed, for a short dash, than any other animal in that country, and I have often wondered how it would fare in a race with a Mongolian gazelle. Unfortunately, conditions in Africa are not favorable for the use of automobiles in hunting, and no actual facts as to the speed of the cheetah are available.

At this camp, and during the journey back to Urga, we had many glorious hunts. Each one held its own individual fascination, for no two were just alike; and every day we learned something new about the life history of the Mongolian antelope. We needed specimens for a group in the new Hall of Asiatic Life in the American Museum of Natural History, as well as a series representing all ages of both males and females for scientific study. When we returned to Urga we had them all.

The hunting of large game was only one aspect of our work. We usually returned to camp about two o'clock in the afternoon. As soon as tiffin had been eaten my wife worked at her photography, while I busied myself over the almost innumerable details of the preparation and cataloguing of our specimens. About six o'clock, accompanied by the two Chinese taxidermists carrying bags of traps, we would leave the tents. Sometimes we would walk several miles, meanwhile carefully scrutinizing the ground for holes or traces of mammal workings, and set eighty or one hundred traps. We might find a colony of meadow voles (*Microtus*) where dozens of "runways" betrayed their presence, or discover the burrows of the desert hamster (*Cricetulus*). These little fellows, not larger than a house mouse, have their tiny feet enveloped in soft fur, like the slippers of an Eskimo baby.

As we walked back to camp in the late afternoon, we often saw a kangaroo rat (*Alactaga mongolica?*) jumping across the plain, and when we had driven it into a hole, we could be sure to catch it in a trap the following morning. They are gentle little creatures, with huge, round eyes, long, delicate ears, and tails tufted at the end like the feathers on an arrow's shaft. The name expresses exactly what they are like— diminutive kangaroos—but, of course, they are rodents and not marsupials. During the glacial period of the early Pleistocene, about one hundred thousand years ago, we know from fossil remains that there were great invasions into Europe of most of these types of tiny mammals, which we were catching during this delightful summer on the Mongolian plains.

After two months we regretfully turned back toward Urga. Our summer was to be divided between the plains on the south and the forests to the north of the sacred city, and the first half of the work had been completed. The results had been very satisfactory, and our boxes contained five hundred specimens; but our hearts were sad. The wide sweep of the limitless, grassy sea, the glorious morning rides, and the magic of the starlit nights had filled our blood. Even the lure of the unknown forests could not make us glad to go, for the plains had claimed us as their own.

CHAPTER X
AN ADVENTURE IN THE LAMA CITY

Late on a July afternoon my wife and I stood disconsolately in the middle of the road on the outskirts of Urga. We had halted because the road had ended abruptly in a muddy river. Moreover, the river was where it had no right to be, for we had traveled that road before and had found only a tiny trickle across its dusty surface. We were disconsolate because we wished to camp that night in Urga, and there were abundant signs that it could not be done.

At least the Mongols thought so, and we had learned that what a Mongol does not do had best "give us pause." They had accepted the river with Oriental philosophy and had made their camps accordingly. Already a score of tents dotted the hillside, and *argul* fires were smoking in the doorways. Hundreds of carts were drawn up in an orderly array while a regiment of oxen wandered about the hillside or sleepily chewed their cuds beside the loads. In a few hours or days or weeks the river would disappear, and then they would go on to Urga. Meanwhile, why worry?

Two adventurous spirits, with a hundred camels, tried to cross. We watched the huge beasts step majestically into the water, only to huddle together in a yellow-brown mass when they reached midstream. All their dignity fled, and they became merely frightened mountains of flesh amid a chaos of writhing necks and wildly switching tails.

But stranger still was a motor car standing on a partly submerged island between two branches of the torrent. We learned later that its owners had successfully navigated the first stream and entered the second. A flooded carburetor had resulted, and ere the car was again in running order, the water had risen sufficiently to maroon them on the island.

My wife and I both lack the philosophical nature of the Oriental, and it was a sore trial to camp within rifle shot of Urga. But we did not dare leave our carts, loaded with precious specimens, to the care of servants and the curiosity of an ever increasing horde of Mongols.

For a well-nigh rainless month we had been hunting upon the plains, while only one hundred and fifty miles away Urga had had an almost daily deluge. In mid-summer heavy rain-clouds roll southward to burst against "God's Mountain," which rears its green-clad summits five thousand feet above the valley. Then it is only a matter of hours before every streamlet becomes a swollen torrent. But they subside as quickly as they rise, and the particular river which barred our road had lost its menace before the sun had risen in a cloudless morning sky. All the valley seemed in motion. We joined the motley throng of camels, carts, and horsemen; and even the motor car coughed and wheezed its way to Urga under the stimulus of two bearded Russians.

We made our camp on a beautiful bit of lawn within a few hundred yards of one of the most interesting of all the Urga temples. It is known to the foreigners in the city as "God's Brother's House," for it was the residence of the Hutukhtu's late brother. The temple presents a bewildering collection of carved gables and gayly painted pavilions flaunting almost every color of the rainbow. Yvette and I were consumed with curiosity to see what was contained within the high palisades which surround the buildings. We knew it would be impossible to obtain permission for her to go inside, and one evening as we were walking along the walls we glanced through the open gate. No one was in sight and from somewhere in the far interior we heard the moaning chant of many voices. Evidently the lamas were at their evening prayers.

We stepped inside the door intending only to take a rapid look. The entire court was deserted, so we slipped through the second gate and stood just at the entrance of the main temple, the "holy of holies." In the half darkness we could see the tiny points of yellow light where candles burned before the altar. On either side was a double row of kneeling lamas, their wailing chant broken by the clash of cymbals and the boom of drums.

Beside the temple were a hideous foreign house and an enormous *yurt*—evidently the former residences of "God's Brother"; in the corners of the compound were ornamental pavilions painted green and red. Except for these, the court was empty.

PLATE X

Tibetan yaks

Our caravan crossing the Terelche River

Suddenly there was a stir among the lamas, and we dashed away like frightened rabbits, dodging behind the gateposts until we were safe outside. It was not until some days later that we learned what a really dangerous thing it was to do, for the temple is one of the holiest in Urga, and in it women are never allowed. Had a Mongol seen us, our camp would have been stormed by a mob of frenzied lamas.

A few days later we had an experience which demonstrates how quickly trouble can arise where religious superstitions are involved. My wife and I had put the motion picture camera in one of the carts and, with our Mongol driving, went to the summit of the hill above the Lama City to film a panoramic view of Urga. We, ourselves, were on horseback. After getting the pictures, we drove down the main street of the city and stopped before the largest temple, which I had photographed several times before.

As soon as the motion picture machine was in position, about five hundred lamas gathered about us. It was a good-natured crowd, however, and we had almost finished work, when a "black Mongol" (i.e., one with a queue, not a lama) pushed his way among the priests and began to harangue them violently. In a few moments he boldly grasped me by the arm. Fearing that trouble might arise, I smiled and said, in Chinese, that we were going away. The Mongol began to gesticulate wildly and attempted to pull me with him farther into the crowd of lamas, who also were becoming excited. I was being separated from Yvette, and realizing that it would be dangerous to get far away from her, I suddenly wrenched my arm free and threw the Mongol to the ground; then I rushed through the line of lamas surrounding Yvette, and we backed up against the cart.

I had an automatic pistol in my pocket, but it would have been suicide to shoot except as a last resort. When a Mongol "starts anything" he is sure to finish it; he is not like a Chinese, who will usually run at the first shot. We stood for at least three minutes with that wall of scowling brutes ten feet away. They were undecided what to do and were only waiting for a leader to close in. One huge beast over six feet tall was just in front of me, and as I stood with my fingers crooked about the trigger of the automatic in my pocket, I thought, "If you start, I'm going to nail you anyway."

Just at this moment of indecision our Mongol leaped on my wife's pony, shouted that he was going to Duke Loobitsan Yangsen, an influential friend of ours, and dashed away. Instantly attention turned from us to him. Fifty men were on horseback in a second, flying after him at full speed. I climbed into the cart, shouting to Yvette to jump on Kublai Khan and run; but she would not leave me. At full speed we dashed down the hill, the plunging horses scattering lamas right and left. Our young Mongol had saved us from a situation which momentarily might have become critical.

At the entrance to the main street of Urga below the Lama City I saw the black Mongol who had started all the trouble. I jumped to the ground, seized him by the collar and one leg, and attempted to throw him into the cart for I had a little matter to settle with him which could best be done to my satisfaction where we were without spectators.

At the same instant a burly policeman, wearing a saber fully five feet long, seized my horse by the bridle. At the black Mongol's instigation (who, I discovered, was himself a policeman) he had been waiting to arrest us when we came into the city. Since it was impossible to learn what had caused the trouble, Yvette rode to Andersen, Meyer's compound to bring back Mr. Olufsen and his interpreter. She found the whole courtyard swarming with excited Mongol soldiers. A few moments later Olufsen arrived, and we were allowed to return to his house on parole. Then he visited the Foreign Minister, who telephoned the police that we were not to be molested further.

We could never satisfactorily determine what it was all about for every one had a different story. The most plausible explanation was as follows. Russians had been rather *persona non grata* in Urga since the collapse of the empire, and the Mongols were ready to annoy them whenever it was possible to do so and "get away with it." All foreigners are supposed to be Russians by the average native and, when the black Mongol discovered us using a strange machine, he thought it an excellent opportunity to "show off" before the lamas. Therefore, he told them that we were casting a spell over the great temple by means of the motion picture camera which I was swinging up and down and from side to side. This may not be the true explanation of the trouble but at least it was the one which sounded most logical to us.

Our lama had been caught in the city, and it was with difficulty that we were able to obtain his release. The police charged that he tried to escape when they ordered him to stop. He related how they had slapped his face and pulled his ears before they allowed him to leave the jail, and he was a very much frightened young man when he appeared at Andersen, Meyer's compound. However, he was delighted to have escaped so easily, as he had had excellent prospects of spending a week or two in one of the prison coffins.

The whole performance had the gravest possibilities, and we were exceedingly fortunate in not having been seriously injured or killed. By playing upon their superstitions, the black Mongol had so inflamed the lamas that they were ready for anything. I should never have allowed them to separate me from my wife and, to prevent it, probably would have had to use my pistol. Had I begun to shoot, death for both of us would have been inevitable.

The day that we arrived in Urga from the plains we found the city flooded. The great square in front of the horse market was a chocolate-colored lake; a brown torrent was rushing down the main street; and every alley was two feet deep in water, or a mass of liquid mud. It was impossible to walk without wading to the knees and even our horses floundered and slipped about, covering us with mud and water. The river valley, too, presented quite a different picture than when we had seen it last. Instead of open sweeps of grassland dotted with an occasional *yurt*, now there were hundreds of felt dwellings interspersed with tents of white or blue. It was like the encampment of a great army, or a collection of huge beehives.

Most of the inhabitants were Mongols from the city who had pitched their *yurts* in the valley for the summer. Although the wealthiest natives seem to feel that for the reception of guests their "position" demands a foreign house, they seldom live in it. Duke Loobitsan Yangsen had completed his mansion the previous winter. It was built in Russian style and furnished with an assortment of hideous rugs and foreign furniture which made one shiver. But in the yard behind the house his *yurt* was pitched, and there he lived in comfort.

Loobitsan was a splendid fellow—one of the best types of Mongol aristocrats. From the crown of his finely molded head to the toes of his pointed boots, he was every inch a duke. I saw him in his house one day reclining on a hang while he received half a dozen minor officials, and his manner of quiet dignity and conscious power recalled accounts of the Mongol princes as Marco Polo saw them.

Loobitsan liked foreigners and one could always find a cordial reception in his compound. He spoke excellent Chinese and was unusually well educated for a Mongol.

Although he was in charge of the customs station at Mai-ma-cheng and owned considerable property, which he rented to the Chinese for vegetable gardens, his chief wealth was in horses. In Mongolia a man's worldly goods are always measured in horses, not in dollars. When he needs cash he sells a pony or two and buys more if he has any surplus silver. His bank is the open plain; his herdsmen are the guardians of his riches.

Loobitsan's wife, the duchess, was a nice-looking woman who seemed rather bored with life. She rejoiced in two gorgeous strings of pearls, which on state occasions hung from the silver-encrusted horns of hair to the shoulders of her brocade jacket. Ordinarily she appeared in a loose red gown and hardly looked regal.

Loobitsan had never seen Peking and was anxious to go. When General Hsu Shu-tseng made his *coup d'etat* in November, 1919, Mr. Larsen and Loobitsan came to the capital as representatives of the Hutukhtu, and one day, as my wife was stepping into a millinery shop on Rue Marco Polo, she met him dressed in all his Mongol splendor. But he was so closely chaperoned by Chinese officials that he could not enjoy himself. I saw Larsen not long afterward, and he told me that Loobitsan was already pining for the open plains of his beloved Mongolia.

In mid-July, when we returned to Urga, the vegetable season was at its height. The Chinese, of course, do all the gardening; and the splendid radishes, beets, onions, carrots, cabbages, and beans, which were brought every day to market, showed the wonderful possibilities for development along these lines. North of the Bogdo-ol there is a superabundance of rain and vegetables grow so rapidly in the rich soil that they are deliciously sweet and tender, besides being of enormous size. While we were on the plains our food had consisted largely of meat and we reveled in the change of diet. We wished often for fruit but that is nonexistent in Mongolia except a few, hard, watery pears, which merchants import from China.

Mr. Larsen was in Kalgan for the summer but Mr. Olufsen turned over his house and compound for our work. I am afraid we bothered him unmercifully, yet his good nature was unfailing and he was never too busy to assist us in the innumerable details of packing the specimens we had obtained upon the plains and in preparing for our trip into the forests north of Urga. It is men like him who make possible scientific work in remote corners of the world.

CHAPTER XI
MONGOLS AT HOME

Until we left Urga the second time Mongolia, to us, had meant only the Gobi Desert and the boundless, rolling plains. When we set our faces northward we found it was also a land of mountains and rivers, of somber forests and gorgeous flowers.

A new forest always thrills me mightily. Be it of stately northern pines, or a jungle tangle in the tropics, it is so filled with glamour and mystery that I enter it with a delightful feeling of expectation. There is so much that is concealed from view, it is so pregnant with the possibility of surprises, that I am as excited as a child on Christmas morning.

The forests of Mongolia were by no means disappointing. We entered them just north of Urga where the Siberian life zone touches the plains of the central Asian region and the beginnings of a new fauna are sharply delineated by the limit of the trees. We had learned that the Terelche River would offer a fruitful collecting ground. It was only forty miles from Urga and the first day's trip was a delight. We traveled northward up a branch valley enclosed by forested hills and carpeted with flowers. Never had we seen such flowers! Acre after acre of bluebells, forget-me-nots, daisies, buttercups, and cowslips converted the entire valley into a vast "old-fashioned garden," radiantly beautiful. Our camp that night was at the base of a mountain called the Da Wat which shut us off from the Terelche River.

On the second morning, instead of golden sunshine, we awoke to a cloud-hung sky and floods of rain. It was one of those days when everything goes wrong; when with all your heart you wish to swear but instead you must smile and smile and keep on smiling. No one wished to break camp in the icy deluge but there were three marshes between us and the Terelche River which were bad enough in dry weather. A few hours of rain would make them impassable, perhaps for weeks.

My wife and I look back upon that day and the next as one of our few, real hardships. After eight hours of killing work, wet to the skin and almost frozen, we crossed the first dangerous swamp and reached the summit of the mountain. Then the cart, with our most valuable possessions, plunged off the road on a sharp descent and crashed into the forest below. Chen and I escaped death by a miracle and the other Chinese taxidermist, who was safe and sound, promptly had hysterics. It was discouraging, to say the least. We camped in the gathering darkness on a forty-five-degree slope in mud twelve inches deep. Next day we gathered up our scattered belongings, repaired the cart, and reached the river.

I had a letter from Duke Loobitsan Yangsen to a famous old hunter, Tserin Dorchy by name, who lives in the Terelche region. He had been gone for six days on a shooting trip when we came into the beautiful valley where his *yurts* were pitched, but his wife welcomed us with true Mongolian hospitality and a great dish of cheese. Our own camp we made just within the forest, a mile away.

For a week we hunted and trapped in the vicinity, awaiting Tserin Dorchy's return. Our arrival created a deal of interest among the half dozen families in the neighborhood and, after each had paid a formal call, they apparently agreed that we were worthy of being accepted into their community. We were nomads for the time, just as they are for life. We had pitched our tents in the forest, as they had erected their *yurts* in the meadow beside the river. When the biting winds of winter swept the valley a few months later they would move, with all their sheep and goats, to the shelter of the hills and we would seek new hunting grounds.

Before many days we learned all the valley gossip. Moreover, we furnished some ourselves for one of the Chinese taxidermists became enamored of a Mongol maiden. There were two of them, to be exact, and they both "vamped" him persistently. The toilettes with which they sought to allure him were marvels of brilliance, and one of them actually scrubbed her little face and hands with a cake of my yellow, scented soap.

Our servant's affections finally centered upon the younger girl and I smiled paternally upon the wild-wood romance. Every night, with a sheepish grin, Chen would ask to borrow a pony. The responsibilities of chaperones sat lightly on our shoulders, but sometimes my wife and I would wander out to the edge of the forest and watch him to the bottom of the hill. Usually his love was waiting and they would ride off together in the moonlight—where, we never asked!

But we could not blame the boy—those Mongolian nights were made for lovers. The marvel of them we hold among our dearest memories. Wherever we may be, the fragrance of pine trees or the sodden smell of a marsh carries us back in thought to the beautiful valley and fills our hearts again with the glory of its clear, white nights.

No matter what the day brought forth, we looked forward to the evening hunt as best of all. As we trotted our ponies homeward through the fresh, damp air we could watch the shadows deepen in the somber masses of the forest, and on the hilltops see the ragged silhouettes of sentinel pines against the rose glow of the sky. Ribbons of mist, weaving in and out above the stream, clothed the alders in ghostly silver and rested in billowy masses upon the marshes. Ere the moon had risen, the stars blazed out like tiny lanterns in the sky. Over all the valley there was peace unutterable.

We were soon admitted to a delightful comradeship with the Mongols of our valley. We shared their joys and sorrows and nursed their minor ills. First to seek our aid was the wife of the absent hunter, Tserin Dorchy. She rode up one day with a two-year-old baby on her arm. The little fellow was badly infected with eczema, and for three weeks one of the lamas in the tiny temple near their *yurt* had been mumbling prayers and incantations in his behalf, without avail. Fortunately, I had a supply of zinc ointment and before the month was ended the baby was almost well. Then came the lama with his bill "for services rendered," and Tserin Dorchy contributed one hundred dollars to his priestly pocket. A young Mongol with a dislocated shoulder was my next patient, and when I had made him whole, the lama again claimed the credit and collected fifty dollars as the honorarium for his prayers. And so it continued throughout the summer; I made the cures, and the priest got the fees.

Although the Mongols all admitted the efficacy of my foreign medicines, nevertheless they could not bring themselves to dispense with the lama and his prayers. Superstition was too strong and fear that the priest would send an army of evil spirits flocking to their *yurts* if they offended him brought the money, albeit reluctantly, from their pockets. Although the lama never proposed a partnership arrangement, as I thought he might have done, he spent much time about our camp and often brought us bowls of curded milk and cheese. He was a wandering priest and not a permanent resident of the valley, but he evidently decided not to wander any farther until we, too, should leave, for he was with us until the very end.

A short time after we had made our camp near the Terelche River a messenger arrived from Urga with a huge package of mail. In it was a copy of *Harper's Magazine* containing an account of a flying visit which I had made to Urga in September, 1918.[1] There were half a dozen Mongols near our tent, among whom was Madame Tserin Dorchy. I explained the pictures to the hunter's wife in my best Chinese while Yvette "stood by" with her camera and watched results. Although the woman had visited Urga several times she had never seen a photograph or a magazine and for ten minutes there was no reaction. Then she recognized a Mongol headdress similar to her own. With a gasp of astonishment she pointed it out to the others and burst into a perfect torrent of guttural expletives. A picture of the great temple at Urga, where she once had gone to worship, brought forth another volume of Mongolian adjectives and her friends literally fought for places in the front row.

News travels quickly in Mongolia and during the next week men and women rode in from *yurts* forty or fifty miles away to see that magazine. I will venture to say that no American publication ever received more appreciation or had a more picturesque audience than did that copy of *Harper's*.

The absent Tserin Dorchy returned one day when I was riding down the valley with his wife. We saw two strange figures on horseback emerging from the forest, each with a Russian rifle on his back. Their saddles were strung about with half-dried skins—four roebuck, a musk deer, a moose, and a pair of elk antlers in the "velvet."

---

[1] *Harper's Magazine*, June, 1919, pp. 1-16.

PLATE XI

Our base camp at the edge of the forest

The Mongol village of the Terelche Valley

With a joyful shout Madame Tserin Dorchy rode toward her husband. He was an oldish man, of fifty-five years perhaps, with a face as dried and weather-beaten as the leather beneath his saddle. He may have been glad to see her but his only sign of greeting was a "*sai*" and a nod to include us both. Her pleasure was undisguised, however, and as we rode down the valley she chattered volubly between the business of driving in half a dozen horses and a herd of sheep. The monosyllabic replies of the hunter were delivered in a voice which seemed to come from a long way off or from out of the earth beneath his pony's feet. I was interested to see what greeting there would be upon his arrival at the *yurt*. His two daughters and his infant son were waiting at the door but he had not even a word for them and only a pat upon the head for the baby.

All Mongols are independent but Tserin Dorchy was an extreme in every way. He ruled the half dozen families in the valley like an autocrat. What he commanded was done without a question. I was anxious to get away and announced that we would start the day after his arrival. "No," said he, "we will go two days from now." Argument was of no avail. So far as he was concerned, the matter was closed. When it came to arranging wages he stated his terms, which were exorbitant. I could accept them or not as I pleased; he would not reduce his demands by a single copper.

As a matter of fact, offers of money make little impression upon the ordinary Mongols. They produce well-nigh everything they need for they dress in sheepskins during the winter and eat little else than mutton. When they want cloth, tea, or ammunition, they simply sell a sheep or a pony or barter with the Chinese merchants.

We found that the personal equation enters very largely into any dealings with a Mongol. If he likes you, remuneration is an incident. If he is not interested, money does not tempt him. His independence is a product of the wild, free life upon the plains. He relies entirely upon himself for he has learned that in the struggle for existence, it is he himself that counts. Of the Chinaman, the opposite is true. His life is one of the community and he depends upon his family and his village. He is gregarious above all else and he hates to live alone. In this dependence upon his fellow men he knows that money counts—and there is very little that a Chinaman will not do for money.

On one of his trips across Mongolia, Mr. Coltman's car became badly mired within a stone's throw of a Mongol *yurt*. Two or three oxen were grazing in front of the house and Coltman asked the native to pull his car out of the mud. The Mongol, who was comfortably smoking his pipe in the sun, was not at all interested in the matter, but finally remarked casually that he would do it for eight dollars. There was no argument. Eight dollars was what he said, and eight dollars it would have to be or he would not move. The entire operation of dragging the car to firm ground consumed just four minutes. But this instance was an exception for usually a Mongol is the very essence of good nature and is ready to assist whenever a traveler is in difficulty.

Tserin Dorchy's independence kept us in a constant state of irritation for it was manifested in a dozen different ways. We would gladly have dispensed with his services but his word was law in the community and, if he had issued a "bull" against us, we could not have obtained another man. For all his age, he was an excellent hunter and we came to be good friends.

The old man's independence once led him into serious trouble. He had often looked at the Bogdo-ol with longing eyes and had made short excursions, without his gun, into its sacred forests. On one of these trips he saw a magnificent elk with antlers such as he had never dreamed were carried by any living animal. He could not forget that deer. Its memory was a thorn that pricked him wherever else he hunted. Finally he determined to have it, even if Mongolian law and the Lama Church had proclaimed it sacred.

Toward the end of July, when he deemed the antlers just ripe for plucking, he slipped into the forest during the night and climbed the mountain. After two days he killed the elk. But the lamas who patrol "God's Mountain" had heard the shot and drove him into a great rock-strewn gorge where they lost his trail. Believing that he was still within hearing distance, they shouted to one another that it was useless to hunt longer and that they had best return. Then they concealed themselves and awaited results. An hour later Tserin Dorchy crawled out from under a bowlder directly into their hands.

He had been well-nigh killed before the lamas brought him down to Urga and was still unconscious when they dumped him unceremoniously into one of the prison coffins. He was sentenced to remain a year; but the old man would not have lived a month if Duke Loobitsan Yangsen, with whom he had often hunted, had not obtained his release. His independent spirit is by no means chastened, however, and I feel sure that he will shoot another deer on the Bogdo-ol before he dies!

Three days after his return home, my wife and I left with him and three other Mongols on our first real hunt. Our equipment consisted only of sleeping bags and such food as could be carried on our horses; it was a time when living "close to nature" was really necessary. Eight miles away we stopped at the entrance to a tiny valley. By arranging a bit of canvas over the low branches of a larch tree we prepared a shelter for ourselves and another for the hunters.

In fifteen minutes camp was ready and a fire blazing. When a huge iron basin of water had begun to warm one of the Mongols threw in a handful of brick tea, which resembled nothing so much as powdered tobacco. After the black fluid had boiled vigorously for ten minutes each one filled his wooden eating bowl, put in a great chunk of rancid butter, and then a quantity of finely-ground meal. This is what the Tibetans call *tsamba*, and the buttered tea was prepared exactly as we had seen the Tibetans make it. The *tsamba*, however, was only to enable them to "carry on" until we killed some game; for meat is the Mongols' "staff of life," and they care little for anything except animal food.

The evening hunt yielded no results. Two of the Mongols had missed a bear, I had seen a roebuck, and the old man had lost a wounded musk deer on the mountain ridge above the camp. But the game was there and we knew where to find it on the morrow. In the gray light of early morning Tserin Dorchy and I rode up the valley through the dew-soaked grass. Once the old man stopped to examine the rootings of a *ga-hai* (wild boar), then he continued steadily along the stream bed. In the half-gloom of the forest the bushes and trees seemed flat and colorless but suddenly the sun burned through an horizon cloud, flooding the woods with golden light. The whole forest seemed instantly to awaken. It was as though we had come into a dimly lighted room and touched an electric switch. The trees and bushes assumed a dozen subtle shades of green, and the flowers blazed like jewels in the gorgeous wood-land carpet.

I should have liked to spend the morning in the forest but we knew the deer were feeding in the open. On foot we climbed upward through knee-high grass to the summit of a hill. There seemed nothing living in the meadow but as we walked along the ridge a pair of grouse shot into the air followed by half a dozen chicks which buzzed away like brown bullets to the shelter of the trees. We crossed a flat depression and rested for a moment on a rounded hilltop. Below us a new valley sloped downward, bathed in sunshine. Tserin Dorchy wandered slowly to the right while I studied the edge of a marsh with my glasses.

Suddenly I heard the muffled beat of hoofs. Jerking the glasses from my eyes I saw a huge roebuck, crowned with a splendid pair of antlers, bound into view not thirty feet away. For the fraction of a second he stopped, with his head thrown back, then dashed along the hillside. That instant of hesitation gave me just time to seize my rifle, catch a glimpse of the yellow-red body through the rear sight, and fire as he disappeared. Leaping to my feet, I saw four slender legs waving in the air. The bullet had struck him in the shoulder and he was down for good.

My heart pounded with exultation as I lifted his magnificent head. He was the finest buck I had ever seen and I gloated over his body as a miser handles his gold. And gold, shining in the sunlight, was never more beautiful than his spotless summer coat.

Right where he lay upon the hillside, amid a veritable garden of bluebells, daisies, and yellow roses, was the setting for the group we wished to prepare in the American Museum of Natural History. He would be its central figure for his peer could not be found in all Mongolia.

As I stood there in the brilliant sunlight, mentally planning the group, I thought how fortunate I was to have been born a naturalist. A sportsman shoots a deer and takes its head; later, it hangs above his fireplace or in the trophy room. If he be one of imagination, in years to come it will bring back to him the feel of the morning air, the fragrance of the pine trees, and the wild thrill of exultation as the buck went down. But it is a memory picture only and limited to himself. The mounted head can never bring to others the smallest part of the joy he felt and the scene he saw.

The naturalist shares his pleasure and, after all, it is largely that which counts. When the group is constructed in the Museum under his direction he can see reproduced with fidelity and in minutest detail this hidden corner of the world. He can share with thousands of city dwellers the joy of his hunt and teach them something of the animals he loves and the lands they call their own.

To his scientific training he owes another source of pleasure. Every animal is a step in the solution of some one of nature's problems. Perhaps it is a new discovery, a species unknown to science. Asia is full of such surprises—I have already found many. Be the specimen large or small, if it has fallen to your trap or rifle, there is the thrill of knowing that you have traced one more small line on the white portion of nature's map.

While I was gazing at the fallen buck Tserin Dorchy stood like a statue on the hilltop, scanning the forest and valley with the hope that my shot had disturbed another animal. In a few moments he came down to me. The old man had lost some of his accustomed calm and, with thumb upraised, murmured, "*Sai, sai.*" Then he gave, in vivid pantomime, a recital of how he suddenly surprised the buck feeding just below the hill crest and how he had seen me jerk the glasses from my eyes and shoot.

Sitting down beside the deer we went through the ceremony of a smoke. Then Tserin Dorchy eviscerated the animal, being careful to preserve the heart, liver, stomach, and intestines. Like all other Orientals with whom I have hunted, the Mongols boiled and ate the viscera as soon as we reached camp and seemed to consider them an especial delicacy.

Some weeks later we killed two elk and Tserin Dorchy inflated and dried the intestines. These were to be used as containers for butter and mutton fat. After tanning the stomach he manufactured from it a bag to contain milk or other liquids. His wife showed me some really beautiful leather which she had made from roebuck skins. Tanning hides and making felt were the only strictly Mongolian industries which we observed in the region visited by our expedition. The Mongols do a certain amount of logging and charcoal burning and in the autumn they cut hay; but with these exceptions we never saw them do any work which could not be done from horseback.

Our first hunting trip lasted ten days and in the following months there were many others. We became typical nomads, spending a day or two in some secluded valley only to move again to other hunting grounds. For the time we were Mongols in all essentials. The primitive instincts, which lie just below the surface in us all, responded to the subtle lure of nature and without an effort we slipped into the care-free life of these children of the woods and plains.

We slept at night under starlit skies in the clean, fresh forest; the first gray light of dawn found us stealing through the dew-soaked grass on the trail of elk, moose, boar or deer; and when the sun was high, like animals, we spent the hours in sleep until the lengthening shadows sent us out again for the evening hunt. In those days New York seemed to be on another planet and very, very far away. Happiness and a great peace was ours, such as those who dwell in cities can never know.

In the midst of our second hunt the Mongols suddenly announced that they must return to the Terelche Valley. We did not want to go, but Tserin Dorchy was obdurate. With the limited Chinese at our command we could not learn the reason, and at the base camp Lü, "the interpreter," was wholly incoherent. "To-morrow, plenty Mongol come," he said. "Riding pony, all same Peking. Two men catch hold, both fall down." My wife was perfectly sure that he had lost his mind, but by a flash of intuition I got his meaning. K was to be a field meet. "Riding pony, all same Peking" meant races, and "two men catch hold, both fall down" could be nothing else than wrestling. I was very proud of myself, and Lü was immensely relieved.

Athletic contests are an integral part of the life of every Mongol community, as I knew, and the members of our valley family were to hold their annual games. At Urga, in June, the great meet which the Living God blesses with his presence is an amazing spectacle, reminiscent of the pageants of the ancient emperors. All the *élite* of Mongolia gather on the banks of the Tola River, dressed in their most splendid robes, and the archery, wrestling, and horse racing are famous throughout the East.

This love of sport is one of the most attractive characteristics of the Mongols. It is a common ground on which a foreigner immediately has a point of contact. The Chinese, on the contrary, despise all forms of physical exercise. They consider it "bad form," and they do not understand any sport which calls for violent exertion. They prefer to take a quiet walk, carrying their pet bird in a cage for an airing; to play a game of cards; or, if they must travel, to loll back in a sedan chair, with the curtains drawn and every breath of air excluded.

The Terelche Valley meet was held on a flat strip of ground just below our camp. As my wife and I rode out of the forest, a dozen Mongols swept by, gorgeous in flaming red and streaming peacock plumes. They waved a challenge to us, and we joined them in a wild race to a flag in the center of the field. On the side of the hill sat a row of lamas in dazzling yellow gowns; opposite them were the judges, among whom I recognized Tserin Dorchy, though he was so bedecked, behatted and beribboned that I could hardly realize that it was the same old fellow with whom we had lived in camp. (I presume if he saw me in the clothes of civilization he would be equally surprised.)

In front of the judges, who represented the most respected laity of the community, were bowls of cheese cut into tiny cubes. The spectators consisted of two groups of women, who sat some distance apart in compact masses, the "horns" of their headdresses almost interlocked. Their costumes were marvels of brilliance. They looked like a flock of gorgeous butterflies, which had alighted for a moment on the grass.

The first race consisted of about a dozen ponies, ridden by fourteen-year-old boys and girls. They swept up the valley from the starting point in full run, hair streaming, and uttering wailing yells. The winner was led by two old Mongols to the row of lamas, before whom he prostrated himself twice, and received a handful of cheese. This he scattered broadcast, as he was conducted ceremoniously to the judges, from whom he returned with palms brimming with bits of cheese.

Finally, all the contestants in the races, and half a dozen of the Mongols on horseback, lined up in front of the priests, each one singing a barbaric chant. Then they circled about the lamas, beating their horses until they were in a full run. After the race came wrestling matches. The contestants sparred for holds and when finally clinched, each with a grip on the other's waistband, endeavored to obtain a fall by suddenly heaving. When the last wrestling match was finished, a tall Mongol raised the yellow banner, and followed by every man and boy on horseback, circled about the seated lamas. Faster and faster they rode, yelling like demons, and then strung off across the valley to the nearest *yurt*.

Although the sports in themselves were not remarkable, the scene was picturesque in the extreme. Opposite to the grassy hill the forest-clad mountains rose, tier upon tier, in dark green masses. The brilliant yellow lamas faced by the Mongols in their blazing robes and pointed yellow hats, the women, flashing with "jewels" and silver, the half-wild chant, and the rush of horses, gave a barbaric touch which thrilled and fascinated us. We could picture this same scene seven hundred years ago, for it is an ancient custom which has come down from the days of Kublai Khan. It was as though the veil of centuries had been lifted for a moment to allow us to carry away, in motion pictures, this drama of Mongolian life.

CHAPTER XII
NOMADS OF THE FOREST

Three days after the field meet we left with Tserin Dorchy and two other Mongols for a wapiti hunt. We rode along the Terelche River for three miles, sometimes splashing through the soggy edges of a marsh, and again halfway up a hillside where the ground was firm and hard; then, turning west on a mountain slope, we came to a low plateau which rolled away in undulating sweeps of hush-land between the edges of the dark pine woods. It was a truly boreal landscape; we were on the edge of the forest, which stretches in a vast, rolling sea of green far beyond the Siberian frontier.

From the summit of the table-land we descended between dark walls of pine trees to a beautiful valley filled with parklike openings. Just at dark Tserin Dorchy turned abruptly into the stream and crossed to a pretty grove of spruces on a little island formed by two branches of the river. It was as secluded as a cavern, and made an ideal place in which to camp. A hundred feet away the tent was invisible and, save for the tiny wreaths of smoke which curled above the tree-tops, there was no sign of our presence there.

After dinner Tserin Dorchy shouldered a pack of skins and went to a "salt lick" in a meadow west of camp to spend the night. He returned in the first gray light of dawn, just as I was making coffee, and reported that he had heard wapiti barking, but that no animals had visited the lick. He directed me to go along the hillsides north of camp, while the Mongol hunters struck westward across the mountains.

I had not been gone an hour, and had just worked across the lower end of a deep ravine, when I heard a wapiti bark above and behind me. It was a hoarse roar, exactly like a roebuck, except that it was deeper toned and louder. I was thrilled as though by an electric current. It seemed very far away, much farther than it really was, and as I crept to the summit of a ridge a splendid bull wapiti broke through the underbrush. He had been feeding in the bottom of the ravine and saw my head instantly as it appeared above the sky line. There was no chance to shoot because of the heavy cover; and even when he paused for a moment on the opposite hillside a screen of tree branches was in my way.

Absolutely disgusted with myself, I followed the animal's trail until it was lost in the heavy forest. The wapiti was gone for good, but on the way back to camp I picked up a roebuck which acted as some balm to my injured feelings.

I had climbed to the crest of the mountains enclosing the valley in which we were camped, and was working slowly down the rim of a deep ravine. In my soft leather moccasins I could walk over the springy moss without a sound, and suddenly saw a yellow-red form moving about in a luxurious growth of grass and tinted leaves. My heart missed a beat, for I thought it was a wapiti.

Instantly I dropped behind a bush and, as the animal moved into the open, I saw it was an enormous roebuck bearing a splendid pair of antlers. I watched him for a moment, then aimed low behind the foreleg and fired. The deer bounded into the air and rolled to the bottom of the ravine, kicking feebly; my bullet had burst the heart. It was one of the few times I have ever seen an animal instantly killed with a heart shot for usually they run a few yards, and then suddenly collapse.

The buck was almost as large as the first one I had killed with Tserin Dorchy but it had a twisted right antler. Evidently it had been injured during the animal's youth and had continued to grow at right angles to the head, instead of straight up in the normal way.

When I reached camp I found Yvette busily picking currants in the bushes beside the stream. Her face and hands were covered with red stains and she looked like a very naughty little boy who had run away from school for a day in the woods. Although blueberries grew on every hillside, we never found strawberries, such as the Russians in Urga gather on the Bogdo-ol, and only one patch of raspberries on a burned-off mountain slope; But the currants were delicious when smothered in sugar.

Yvette and I rode out to the spot where I had killed the roebuck to bring it in on Kublai Khan and before we returned the Mongol hunters had reached camp; neither of them had seen game of any kind. During the day we discovered some huge trout in the stream almost at our door. We had no hooks or hues, but the Mongols devised a way to catch the fish which brought us food, although it would have made a sportsman shiver. They built a dam of stones across the stream and one man waded slowly along, beating the water with a branch to drive the trout out of the pools into the ripples; then we dashed into the water and tried to catch them with our hands. At least a dozen got away but we secured three by cornering them among the rocks.

They were huge trout, nearly three feet long. Unfortunately I was not able to preserve any of them and I do not know what species they represented. The Mongols and Chinese often catch the same fish in the Tola River by means of nets and we sometimes bought them in Urga. One, which we put on the scales, weighed nine pounds. Although Ted MacCallie tried to catch them with a fly at Urga he never had any success but they probably would take live bait.

August 20 was our second day in camp. At dawn I was awakened by the patter of rain on the tent and soon it became a steady downpour. There was no use in hunting and I went back to sleep. At seven o'clock Chen, who was fussing about the fire, rushed over to say that he could see two wapiti on the opposite mountain. Yvette and I scrambled out of our sleeping bags just in time to see a doe and a fawn silhouetted against the sky rim as they disappeared over the crest. Half an hour later they returned, and I tried a stalk but I lost them in the fog and rain. Tserin Dorchy believed that the animals had gone into a patch of forest on the other side of the mountain. We tried to drive them out but the only thing that appeared was a four-year-old roebuck which the Mongol killed with a single shot.

We had ridden up the mountain by zigzagging across the slope, but when we started back I was astounded to see Tserin Dorchy keep to his saddle. The wet grass was so slippery that I could not even stand erect and half the time was sliding on my back, while Kublai Khan picked his way carefully down the steep descent. The Mongol never left his horse till we reached camp. Sometimes he even urged the pony to a trot and, moreover, had the roebuck strapped behind his saddle. I would not have ridden down that mountain side for all the deer in Mongolia!

PLATE XII

Wrestlers at Terelche Valley field meet

Women spectators at the field meet

It had begun to rain in earnest by eleven o'clock, and we spent a quiet afternoon. There is a charm about a rainy day when one can read comfortably and let it pour. The steady patter on the tent gives one the delightful sensation of immediately escaping extreme discomfort. There is no pleasure in being warm unless the weather is cold; and one never realizes how agreeable it is to be dry unless the day is wet. This day was very wet indeed. We had a month's accumulation of unopened magazines which a Mongol had brought to our base camp just before we left, so there was no chance of being bored. The fire had been built half under a huge, back-log which kept a cheery glow of coals throughout all the downpour, and Chen made us "*chowdzes*"—delicious little balls of meat mixed with onions and seasoned with Chinese sauce. The Mongols slept and ate and slept some more. We ate and slept and read. Therefore, we were very happy.

The weather during that summer in the forest was a source of constant surprise to us. We had never seen such rapid changes from brilliant sunshine to sheets of rain. For an hour or two the sky might stretch above us like a vast blue curtain flecked with tiny masses of snow-white clouds. Suddenly, a leaden blanket would spread itself over every inch of celestial space, while a rush of rain and wind changed the forest to a black chaos of writhing branches and dripping leaves. In fifteen minutes the storm would sweep across the mountain tops, and the sun would again flood our peaceful valley with the golden light of early autumn.

For autumn had already reached us even though the season was only mid-August. It was like October in New York, and we had nightly frosts which withered the countless flowers and turned the leaves to red and gold. In the morning, when I crossed the meadows to the forest, the grass was white with frost and crackled beneath my feet like delicate threads of spun glass. My moccasins were powdered with gleaming crystals of frozen dew, but at the first touch of sun every twig and leaf and blade of grass began to drip, as though from a heavy rain. My feet and legs waist-high were soaked in half an hour, and at the end of the morning hunt I was as wet as though I had waded a dozen rivers.

One cannot move on foot in northern Mongolia without the certainty of a thorough wetting. When the sun has dried the dew, there are swamps and streamlets in every valley and even far up the mountain slopes. It is the heavy rainfall, the rich soil, and the brilliant sunshine that make northern Mongolia a paradise of luxurious grass and flowers, even though the real summer lasts only from May till August.

Then, the valleys are like an exquisite garden and the woods are ablaze with color. Bluebells, their stalks bending under the weight of blossoms, clothe every hillside in a glorious azure dress bespangled with yellow roses, daisies, and forget-me-nots. But I think I like the wild poppies best of all, for their delicate, fragile beauty is wonderfully appealing. I learned to love them first in Alaska, where their pale, yellow faces look up happily from the storm-swept hills of the Pribilof Islands in the Bering Sea.

Besides its flowers, this northern country is one of exceeding beauty. The dark green forests of spruce, larch and pine, broken now and then by a grove of poplars or silver birches, the secluded valleys and the rounded hills are strangely restful and give one a sense of infinite peace. It is a place to go for tired nerves. Ragged peaks, towering mountains, and yawning chasms, splendid as they are, may be subtly disturbing, engendering a feeling of restlessness and vague depression. There is none of this in the forests of Mongolia. We felt as though we might be happy there all our lives—the mad rush of our other world seemed very far away and not much worth while.

As yet this land has been but lightly touched by the devastating hand of man. A log road cuts the forest here and there and sometimes we saw a train of ox-carts winding through the trees; but the primitive beauty of the mountains remains unmarred, save where a hillside has been swept by fire. In all our wanderings through the forests we saw no evidences of occupation by the Mongols except the wood roads and a few scattered charcoal pits. These were old and moss-grown, and save for ourselves the valleys were deserted.

One morning while I was hunting north of camp, I heard a wapiti roar on the summit of a mountain. I found its tracks in the soft earth of a game trail which wound through forest so dense that I could hardly see a dozen yards. As I stole along the path I heard a sudden sneeze exactly like that of a human being and saw a small, dark animal dash off the trail. I stopped instantly and slowly sank to the ground, kneeling motionless, with my rifle ready. For five minutes I remained there—the silence of the forest broken only by the clucking of a hazel grouse above my head. Then came that sneeze again, sounding even more human than before. I heard a nervous patter of tiny hoofs, and the animal sneezed from the bushes at my right. I kept as motionless as a statue, and the sneezes followed each other in rapid succession, accompanied by impatient stampings and gentle rustlings in the brush. Then I saw a tiny head emerge from behind a leafy screen and a pair of brilliant eyes gazing at me steadily. Very, very slowly I raised the rifle until the stock nestled against my cheek; then I fired quickly.

Running to the spot where the head had been I found a beautiful brown-gray animal lying behind a bush. It was no larger than a half-grown fawn, but on either side of its mouth two daggerlike tusks projected, slender, sharp and ivory white. It was a musk deer—the first living, wild one I had ever seen. Even before I touched the body I inhaled a heavy, not unpleasant, odor of musk and discovered the gland upon the abdomen. It was three inches long and two inches wide, but all the hair on the rump and belly was strongly impregnated with the odor.

These little deer are eagerly sought by the natives throughout the Orient, as musk is valuable for perfume. In Urga the Mongols could sell a "pod" for five dollars (silver) and in other parts of China it is worth considerably more. When we were in Yün-nan we frequently heard of a musk buyer whom the Paris perfumer, Pinaud, maintained in the remote mountain village of Atunzi, on the Tibetan frontier.

Because of their commercial value the little animals are relentlessly persecuted in every country which they inhabit and in some places they have been completely exterminated. Those in Mongolia are particularly difficult to kill, since they live only on the mountain summits in the thickest forests. Indeed, were it not for their insatiable curiosity it would be almost impossible ever to shoot them.

They might be snared, of course, but I never saw any traps or devices for catching animals which the Mongols used; they seem to depend entirely upon their guns. This is quite unlike the Chinese, Koreans, Manchus, Malays, and other Orientals with whom I have hunted, for they all have developed ingenious snares, pitfalls and traps.

The musk sac is present only in the male deer and is, of course, for the purpose of attracting the does. Unfortunately, it is not possible to distinguish the sexes except upon close examination, for both are hornless, and as a result the natives sometimes kill females which they would prefer to leave unmolested.

The musk deer use their tusks for fighting and also to dig up the food upon which they live. I frequently found new pine cones which they had torn apart to get at the soft centers. During the winter they develop an exceedingly long, thick coat of hair which, however, is so brittle that it breaks almost like dry pine needles; consequently, the skins have but little commercial value.

Late one rainy afternoon Tserin Dorchy and I rode into a beautiful valley not far from where we were camped. When well in the upper end, we left our horses and proceeded on foot toward the summit of a ridge on which he had killed a bear a month earlier.

Motioning me to walk to the crest of the ridge from the other side, the old man vanished like a ghost among the trees. When I was nearly at the top I reached the edge of a small patch of burned forest. In the half darkness the charred stumps and skeleton trees were as black as ebony. As I was about to move into the open I saw an object which at first seemed to be a curiously shaped stump. I looked at it casually, then something about it arrested my attention. Suddenly a tail switched nervously and I realized that the "stump" was an enormous wild boar standing head-on, watching me.

I fired instantly, but even as I pressed the trigger the animal moved and I knew that the bullet would never reach its mark. But my brain could not telegraph to my finger quickly enough to stop its action and the boar dashed away unharmed. It was the largest pig I have ever seen. As he stood on the summit of the ridge he looked almost as big as a Mongol pony. It was too dark to follow the animal so I returned to camp, a very dejected man.

I have never been able to forget that boar and I suppose I never shall. Later, I killed others but they can never destroy the memory of that enormous animal as he stood there looking down at me. Had I realized that it was a pig only the fraction of a second sooner it would have been a different story. But that is the fortune of shooting. In no other sport is the line between success and failure so closely drawn; of course, it is that which makes it so fascinating. At the end of a long day's hunt one chance may be given; then all depends on a clear eye, a steady hand and, above all, judgment. In your action in that single golden second rests the success or failure of, perhaps, a season's trip. You may have traveled thousands of miles, spent hundreds of dollars, and had just one shot at the "head of heads."

Some men tell me that they never get excited when they hunt. Thank God, I do. There would be no fun at all for me if I *didn't* get excited. But, fortunately, it all comes after the crucial moment. When the stock of the rifle settles against my cheek and I look across the sights, I am as cold as steel. I can shoot, and keep on shooting, with every brain cell concentrated on the work in hand but when it is done, for better or worse, I get the reaction which makes it all worth while.

One morning, a week after we had been in camp, Tserin Dorchy and I discovered a cow and a calf wapiti feeding in an open forest. It was a delight to see how the old Mongol stalked the deer, slipping from tree to bush, sometimes on his knees or flat on his face in the soft moss carpet. When we were two hundred yards away we drew up behind a stump. I took the cow, while Tserin Dorchy covered the calf and at the sound of our rifles both animals went down for good. I was glad to have them for specimens because we never got a shot at a bull in Mongolia, although twice I lost one by the merest chance. One of our hunters brought in a three-year-old moose a short time after we got the wapiti and another had a long chase after a wounded bear.

It was the first week in September when we returned to the base camp, our ponies heavily loaded with skins and antlers. The Chinese taxidermists under my direction had made a splendid collection of small mammals, and we had pretty thoroughly exhausted the resources of the forests in the Terelche region. Therefore, Yvette and I decided that it would be well to ride into Urga and make arrangements for our return to Peking.

We did the fifty miles with the greatest ease and spent the night with Mamen in Mai-ma-cheng. Next day Mr. and Mrs. MacCallie arrived, much to our delight. They were to spend the winter in Urga on business and they brought a supply of much needed ammunition, photographic plates, traps and my Mannlicher rifle. This equipment had been shipped from New York ten months earlier but had only just reached Peking and been released from the Customs through the heroic efforts of Mr. Guptil.

We had another two weeks' hunting trip before we said good-by to Mongolia but it netted few results. All the valleys, which had been deserted when we were there before, were filled with Mongols cutting hay for the winter feed of their sheep and goats. Of course, every camp was guarded by a dog or two, and their continual barking had driven the moose, elk, and bear far back into the deepest forests where we had no time to follow.

Mr. and Mrs. MacCallie had taken a house in Urga, just opposite the Russian Consulate, and they entertained us while I packed our collections which were stored in Andersen, Meyer's godown. It was a full week's work, for we had more than a thousand specimens. The forests of Mongolia had yielded up their treasures as we had not dared to hope they would, and we left them with almost as much regret as we had left the plains.

October first the specimens started southward on camel back. Kublai Khan, my pony, went with them, while we left in the Chinese Government motor cars. For two hundred miles we rushed over the same plains which, a few months earlier, we had laboriously crossed with our caravan. Every spot was pregnant with delightful memories. At this well we had camped for a week and hunted antelope; in that ragged mass of rocks we had killed a wolf; out on the Turin plain we had trapped twenty-six marmots in an enormous colony.

Those had been glorious days and our hearts were sad as we raced back to Peking and civilization. But one bright spot remained—we need not yet leave our beloved East! Far to the south, in brigand-infested mountains on the edge of China, there dwelt a herd of bighorn sheep, the *argali* of the

Mongols. Among them was a great ram, and we had learned his hiding place. How we got him is another story.

CHAPTER XIII
THE PASSING OF MONGOLIAN MYSTERY

I know of no other country about which there is so much *misinformation* as about Mongolia. Because the Gobi Desert stretches through its center the popular conception appears to be that it is a waste of sand and gravel incapable of producing anything. In the preceding chapters I have attempted to give a picture of the country as we found it and, although our interests were purely zoölogical, I should like to present a few notes regarding its commercial possibilities, for I have never seen a land which is readily accessible and is yet so undeveloped.

Every year the Far East is becoming increasingly important to the Western World, and especially to the people of the United States, for China and its dependencies is the logical place for the investment of American capital. It is the last great undeveloped field, and I am interested in seeing the American business man appreciate the great opportunities which await him in the Orient.

It is true that the Gobi Desert is a part of Mongolia, but only in its western half is it a desolate waste; in the eastern section it gradually changes into a rolling plain covered with "Gobi sage brush" and short bunch grass. When one looks closely one sees that the underlying soil is very fine gravel and sand.

There is little water in this region except surface ponds, which are usually dry in summer, and caravans depend upon wells. The water in the desert area contains some alkali but, except in a few instances, the impregnation is so slight that it is not especially disagreeable to the taste. Mr. Larsen told me that there is no part of the country between Kalgan and Urga in which water cannot be found within ten or twenty feet of the surface. I am not prepared to say what this arid region could be made to produce. Doubtless, from the standpoint of agriculture it would be of little importance but sheep and goats could live upon its summer vegetation, I am sure.

It is difficult to say where the Gobi really begins or ends when crossing it between Kalgan and Urga, for the grasslands both on the south and north merge so imperceptibly into the arid central part that there is no real "edge" to the desert; however, it is safe to take Panj-kiang as the southern margin, and Turin as the northern limit, of the Gobi. Both in the north and south the land is rich and fertile—much like the plains of Siberia or the prairies of Kansas and Nebraska.

Such is the eastern Gobi from June to mid-September. In the winter, when the dried vegetation exposes the surface soil, the whole aspect of the country is changed and then it does resemble the popular conception of a desert. But what could be more desertlike than our north China landscape when frost has stripped away the green clothing of its hills and fields?

The Chinese have already demonstrated the agricultural possibilities in the south and every year they reap a splendid harvest of oats, wheat, millet, buckwheat and potatoes. On the grass-covered meadowlands, both north and south of the Gobi, there are vast herds of sheep, goats, cattle and horses, but they are only a fraction of the numbers which the pasturage could support. The cattle and sheep which are exported through China can be sent to Kalgan "on the hoof," for since grass is plentiful, the animals can graze at night and travel during the day. This very materially reduces the cost of transportation.

Besides the great quantities of beef and mutton which could be raised and marketed in the Orient, America or Europe, thousands of pounds of wool and camel hair could be exported. Of course both of these articles are produced at the present time, but only in limited quantities. In the region where we spent the summer, the Mongols sometimes do not shear their sheep or camels but gather the wool from the ground when it has dropped off in the natural process of shedding. Probably half of it is lost, and the remainder is full of dirt and grass which detracts greatly from its value. Moreover, when it is shipped the impurities add at least twenty per cent to its weight, and the high cost of transportation makes this an important factor. Indeed, under proper development the pastoral resources of Mongolia are almost unlimited.

The Turin-Urga region has another commercial asset in the enormous colonies of marmots which inhabit the country for hundreds of miles to the north, east and west. The marmots are prolific breeders—each pair annually producing six or eight young—and, although their fur is not especially fine, it has always been valuable for coats. Several million marmot pelts are shipped every year from Mongolia, the finest coming from Uliassutai in the west, and were American steel traps introduced the number could be doubled.

Urga is just being discovered as a fur market. Many skins which have been taken well across the Russian frontier are sold in Urga, and as the trade increases it will command a still wider area. Wolves, foxes, lynx, bear, wildcats, sables, martens, squirrels and marmots are brought in by thousands; and great quantities of sheep, goat, cow and antelope hides are sent annually to Kalgan. Several foreign fur houses of considerable importance already have their representatives in Urga and more are coming every year. The possibilities for development in this direction are almost boundless, and I believe that within a very few years Urga will become one of the greatest fur markets of the Orient.

As in the south the Chinese farmer cultivates the grasslands of the Mongols, so in the north the Chinese merchant has assumed the trade. Many firms in Peking and Tientsin have branches in Urga and make huge profits in the sale of food, cloth and other essentials to the Mongols and foreigners and in the export of furs, skins and wool. It is well-nigh impossible to touch business in Mongolia at any point without coming in contact with the Chinese.

All work not connected with animals is assumed by Chinese, for the Mongols are almost useless for anything which cannot be done from the back of a horse. Thus the Chinese have a practical monopoly and they exercise all their prerogatives in the enormous prices which they charge for the slightest service. Mongols and foreigners suffer together in this respect, but there is no alternative—the Chinaman can charge what he pleases, for he knows full well that no one else will do the work.

Although there is considerable mineral wealth in northern Mongolia, up to the present time very little prospecting has been done. For several years a Russian company has carried on successful operations for gold at the Yero mines, between

Urga and Kiakhta on the Siberian frontier, but they have had to import practically all their labor from China. We often passed Chinese in the Gobi Desert walking across Mongolia pushing a wheelbarrow which contained all their earthly belongings. They were on their way to the Yero mines for the summer's work; in the fall they would return on foot the way they had come. Now that Mongolia is once more a part of the Chinese Republic, the labor problem probably will be improved for there will certainly be an influx of Chinese who are anxious to work.

Transportation is the greatest of all commercial factors in the Orient and upon it largely depends the development of any country. In Mongolia the problem can be easily solved. At the present time it rests upon camel caravans, ox and pony carts and upon automobiles for passengers. Camel traffic begins in September and is virtually ended by the first of June. Then their places on the trail are taken by ox- and pony-carts. Camels make the journey from Kalgan to Urga in from thirty to fifty days, but the carts require twice as long. They travel slowly, at best, and the animals must be given time to graze and rest. Of course, they cannot cross the desert when the grass is dry, so that transportation is divided by the season—camels in winter and carts in summer. Each camel carries from four hundred and fifty to five hundred pounds, and the charges for the journey from Kalgan to Urga vary with conditions at from five to fifteen cents (silver) per *cattie* (one and one-third pounds). Thus, by the time goods have reached Urga, their value has increased tremendously.

I can see no reason why motor trucks could not make the trip and am intending to use them on my next expedition. Between Panj-kiang and Turin, the first and third telegraph stations, there is some bad going in spots, but a well made truck with a broad wheel base and a powerful engine certainly could negotiate the sand areas without difficulty. After Turin, where the Gobi may be said to end, the road is like a boulevard.

The motor service for passengers which the Chinese Government maintains between Kalgan and Urga is a branch of the Peking-Suiyuan Railway and has proved successful after some initial difficulties due to careless and inexperienced chauffeurs. Although the service badly needs organization to make it entirely safe and comfortable, still it has been effective even in its crude form.

At the present time a great part of the business which is done with the Mongols is by barter. The Chinese merchants extend credit to the natives for material which they require and accept in return cattle, horses, hides, wool, etc., to be paid at the proper season. In recent years Russian paper *rubles* and Chinese silver have been the currency of the country, but since the war Russian money has so depreciated that it is now practically valueless. Mongolia greatly needs banking facilities and under the new political conditions undoubtedly these will be materially increased.

A great source of wealth to Mongolia lies in her magnificent forests of pine, spruce, larch and birch which stretch away in an almost unbroken line of green to far beyond the Siberian frontier. As yet but small inroads have been made upon these forests, and as I stood one afternoon upon the summit of a mountain gazing over the miles of timbered hills below me, it seemed as though here at least was an inexhaustible supply of splendid lumber. But no more pernicious term was ever coined than "inexhaustible supply!" I wondered, as I watched the sun drop into the somber masses of the forest, how long these splendid hills would remain inviolate. Certainly not many years after the Gobi Desert has been crossed by lines of steel, and railroad sheds have replaced the gold-roofed temples of sacred Urga.

We are at the very beginning of the days of flying, and no land which contains such magnificent spruce can keep its treasure boxes unspoiled for very long. Even as I write, aëroplanes are waiting in Peking to make their first flight across Mongolia. The desert nomads have not yet ceased to wonder at the motor cars which cover as many miles of plain in one day as their camels cross in ten. But what *will* they think when twenty men leave Kalgan at noon and dine in Urga at seven o'clock that night! Seven hundred miles mean very little to us now! The start has been made already and, after all, it is largely that which counts. The automobile has come to stay, we know; and motor trucks will soon do for freight what has already been done for passengers, not only from Kalgan to Urga, but west to Uliassutai, and on to Kobdo at the very edge of the Altai Mountains. Few spots in Mongolia need remain untouched, if commercial calls are strong enough.

Last year the first caravans left Feng-chen with wireless equipment for the eighteen hundred mile journey across Mongolia to Urumchi in the very heart of central Asia. Construction at Urga is well advanced and it will soon begin at Kashgar. When these stations are completed Kobdo in Mongolia, Hami in Chinese Turkestan, and Sian-fu in Shensi will see wireless shafts erected; and old Peking will be in touch with the remotest spots of her far-flung lands at any time by day or night.

These things are not idle dreams—they are hard business facts already in the first stages of accomplishment. Why, then, should the railroad be long delayed? It may be built from Kalgan to Urga, or by way of Kwei-hua-cheng—either route is feasible. It will mean a direct connection between Shanghai, China's greatest port, and Verkhin Udinsk on the Trans-Siberian Railroad via Tientsin, Peking, Kalgan, Urga, Kiakhta. It will shorten the trip to London by at least four days for passengers and freight. It will open for settlement and commercial development a country of boundless possibilities and unknown wealth which for centuries has been all but forgotten.

Less than seven hundred years ago Mongolia well-nigh ruled the world. Her people were strong beyond belief, but her empire crumbled as quickly as it rose, leaving to posterity only a glorious tradition and a land of mystery. The tradition will endure for centuries; but the motor car and aëroplane and wireless have dispelled the mystery forever.

CHAPTER XIV
THE GREAT RAM OF THE SHANSI MOUNTAINS

Away up in northern China, just south of the Mongolian frontier, is a range of mountains inhabited by bands of wild sheep. They are wonderful animals, these sheep, with horns like battering-rams. But the mountains are also populated by brigands and the two do not form an agreeable combination from the sportsman's standpoint.

In reality they are perfectly nice, well-behaved brigands, but occasionally they forget their manners and swoop down upon the caravan road less than a dozen miles away. This is done only when scouts bring word that cargo valuable enough to make it worth while is about to pass. Each time the brigands make a foray a return raid by Chinese soldiers can be expected. Occasionally these are real, "honest-to-goodness" fights, and blood may flow on both sides, but the battle sometimes takes a different form.

With bugles blowing, the soldiers march out to the hills. Through "middle men" the battle ground has been agreed upon, and a "David" is chosen from the soldiers to meet the "Goliath" of the brigands. But David is particularly careful to leave his gun behind, and to have his "sling" well stuffed with rifle shells. Goliath advances to the combat armed only with a bag of silver dollars. Then an even trade ensues—a dollar for a cartridge—and the implement of war changes hands.

The soldiers return to the city with bugles sounding as merrily as when they left. The commander sends a report to Peking of a desperate battle with the brigands. He says that, through the extreme valor of his soldiers, the bandits have been dispersed and many killed; that hundreds of cartridges were expended in the fight; therefore, kindly send more as soon as possible.

All this because the government has an unfortunate way of forgetting to pay its soldiers in the outlying provinces. When no money is forthcoming and none is visible on the horizon, it is not surprising that they take other means to obtain it. "Battles" of this type are by no means exceptions— they are more nearly the rule in many provinces of China.

PLATE XIII

Cave dwellings in north Shansi Province

An Asiatic wapiti

*Harry R. Caldwell and a
Mongolian Bighorn*

But what has all this to do with the wild sheep? Its relation is very intimate, for the presence of brigands in those Shansi mountains has made it possible for the animals to exist. The hunting grounds are only five days' travel from Peking and many foreigners have turned longing eyes toward the mountains. But the brigands always had to be considered. Since Sir Richard Dane, formerly Chief Inspector of the Salt Gabelle, and Mr. Charles Coltman were driven out by the bandits in 1915, the Chinese Government has refused to grant passports to foreigners who wished to shoot in that region.

The brigands themselves cannot waste cartridges at one dollar each on the sheep, so the animals have been allowed to breed unmolested.

Nevertheless, there are not many sheep there. They are the last survivors of great herds which once roamed the mountains of north China. The technical name of the species is *Ovis commosa* (formerly *O. jubata*) and it is one of the group of bighorns known to sportsmen by the Mongol name of *argali*. In size, as well as ancestry, the members of this group are the grandfathers of all the sheep. The largest ram of our Rocky Mountains is a pygmy compared with a full-grown *argali*. Hundreds of thousands of years ago the bighorns, which originated in Asia, crossed into Alaska by way of the Bering Sea, where there was probably a land connection at that time. From Alaska they gradually worked southward, along the mountains of the western coast, into Mexico and Lower California. In the course of time, changed environment developed different species; but the migration route from the Old World to the New is there for all to read.

The supreme trophy of a sportsman's life is the head of a Mongolian bighorn sheep. I think it was Rex Beach who said, "Some men can shoot but not climb. Some can climb but not shoot. To get a sheep you must be able to climb and shoot, too."

For its Hall of Asiatic Life, the American Museum of Natural History needed a group of *argali*. Moreover, we wanted a ram which would fairly represent the species, and that meant a very big one. The Reverend Harry R. Caldwell, with whom I had hunted tiger in south China, volunteered to get them with me. The brigands did not worry us unduly, for we both have had considerable experience with Chinese bandits and we feel that they are like animals—if you don't tease them, they won't bite. In this case the "teasing" takes the form of carrying anything that they could readily dispose of—especially money. I decided that my wife must remain in Peking. She was in open rebellion but there was just a possibility that the brigands might annoy us, and we had determined to have those sheep regardless of consequences.

Although we did not expect trouble, I knew that Harry Caldwell could be relied upon in any emergency. When a man will crawl into a tiger's lair, a tangle of sword grass and thorns, just to find out what the brute has had for dinner; when he will walk into the open in dim light and shoot, with a .22 high-power rifle, a tiger which is just ready to charge; when he will go alone and unarmed into the mountains to meet a band of brigands who have been terrorizing the country, it means that he has more nerve than any one man needs in this life!

After leaving the train at Feng-chen, the journey was like all others in north China; slow progress with a cart over atrocious roads which are either a mass of sticky mud or inches deep in fine brown dust. We had four days of it before we reached the mountains but the trip was full of interest to us both, for along the road there was an ever-changing picture of provincial life. To Harry it was especially illuminating because he had spent nineteen years in south China and had never before visited the north. He began to realize what every one soon learns who wanders much about the Middle Kingdom—that it is never safe to generalize in this strange land. Conditions true of one region may be absolutely unknown a few hundred miles away. He was continually irritated to find that his perfect knowledge of the dialect of Fukien Province was utterly useless. He was well-nigh as helpless as though he had never been in China, for the languages of the north and the south are almost as unlike as are French and German. Even our "boys" who were from Peking had some difficulty in making themselves understood, although we were not more than two hundred miles from the capital.

Instead of hills thickly clothed with sword grass, here the slopes were bare and brown. We were too far north for rice; corn, wheat, and *kaoliang* took the place of paddy fields. Instead of brick-walled houses we found dwellings made of clay like the "adobe" of Mexico and Arizona. Sometimes whole villages were dug into the hillside and the natives were cave dwellers, spending their lives within the earth.

All north China is spread with loess. During the Glacial Period, about one hundred thousand years ago, when in Europe and America great rivers of ice were descending from the north, central and eastern Asia seems to have suffered a progressive dehydration. There was little moisture in the air so that ice could not be formed. Instead, the climate was cold and dry, while violent winds carried the dust in whirling clouds for hundreds upon hundreds of miles, spreading it in ever thickening layers over the hills and plains. Therefore, the "Ice Age" for Europe and America was a "Dust Age" for northeastern Asia.

The inns were a constant source of interest to us both. Their spacious courtyards contrasted strangely with the filthy "hotels" of southern China. In the north all the traffic is by cart, and there must be accommodation for hundreds of vehicles; in the south where goods are carried by boats, coolies, or on donkey back, extensive compounds are unnecessary. Each night, wherever we arrived, we found the courtyard teeming with life and motion. Line after line of laden carts wound in through the wide swinging gates and lined up in orderly array; there was the steady "crunch, crunch, crunch" of feeding animals, shouts for the *jonggweda* (landlord), and good-natured chaffing among the carters. In the great kitchen, which is also the sleeping room, over blazing fires fanned by bellows, pots of soup and macaroni were steaming. On the two great *kangs* (bed platforms), heated from below by long flues radiating outward from the cooking fires, dozens of *mafus* were noisily sucking in their food or already snoring contentedly, rolled in their dusty coats.

Many kinds of folk were there; rich merchants enveloped in splendid sable coats and traveling in padded carts; peddlers with packs of trinkets for the women; wandering doctors selling remedies of herbs, tonics made from deerhorns or tigers' teeth, and wonderful potions of "dragons' bones." Perhaps there was a Buddhist priest or two, a barber, or a tailor. Often a professional entertainer sat cross-legged on the hang telling endless stories or singing for hours at a time in a high-pitched, nasal voice, accompanying himself upon a tiny snake-skin violin. It was like a stage drama of concentrated Chinese country life.

Among this polyglot assembly perhaps there may be a single man who has arrived with a pack upon his back. He is indistinguishable from the other travelers and mingles among the *mafus*, helping now and then to feed a horse or adjust a load. But his ears and eyes are open. He is a brigand scout who is there to learn what is passing on the road. He hears all the gossip from neighboring towns as well as of those many miles away, for the inns are the newspapers of rural China, and it is every one's business to tell all he knows. The scout marks a caravan, then slips away into the mountains to report to the leader of his band. The attack may not take place for many days. While the unsuspecting *mafus* are plodding on their way, the bandits are hovering on the outskirts among the hills until the time is ripe to strike.

I have learned that these brigand scouts are my best protection, for when a foreigner arrives at a country inn all other subjects of conversation lose their interest. Everything about him is discussed and rediscussed, and the scouts discover all there is to know. Probably the only things I ever carry which a bandit could use or dispose of readily, are arms and ammunition. But two or three guns are hardly worth the trouble which would follow the death of a foreigner. The brigands know that there would be no sham battle with Chinese soldiers in that event, for the Legations at Peking have a habit of demanding reparation from the Government and insisting that they get it.

As a *raison d'être* for our trip Caldwell and I had been hunting ducks, geese, and pheasants industriously along the way, and not even the "boys" knew our real destination.

We had looked forward with great eagerness to the Tai Hai, a large lake, where it was said that water fowl congregated in thousands during the spring and fall. We reached the lake the second night after leaving Feng-chen. Darkness had just closed about us when we crossed the summit of a high mountain range and descended into a narrow, winding cut which eventually led us out upon the flat plains of the Tai Hai basin. While we were in the pass a dozen flocks of geese slipped by above our heads, flying very low, the "wedges" showing black against the starlit sky.

With much difficulty we found an inn close beside the lake and, after a late supper, snuggled into our fur bags to be lulled to sleep by that music most dear to a sportsman's heart, the subdued clamor of thousands of water-fowl settling themselves for the night.

At daylight we dressed hurriedly and ran to the lake shore. Harry took a station away from the water at the base of the hills, while I dropped behind three conical mounds which the natives had constructed to obtain salt by evaporation.

I was hardly in position before two geese came straight for me. Waiting until they were almost above my head, I knocked down both with a right and left. The shots put thousands of birds in motion. Flock after flock of geese rose into the air, and long lines of ducks skimmed close to the surface, settling away from shore or on the mud flats near the water's edge.

No more birds came near me, and in fifteen minutes I returned to the inn for breakfast. Harry appeared shortly after with only a mallard duck, for he had guessed wrong as to the direction of the flight, and was entirely out of the shooting.

When the carts had started at eight o'clock Harry and I rode down the shore of the lake to the south, with Chen to hold our horses. The mud flats were dotted with hundreds of ruddy sheldrakes, their beautiful bodies glowing red and gold in the sunlight. A hundred yards from shore half a dozen swans drifted about like floating snow banks, and ducks and geese by thousands rose or settled in the lake. We saw a flock of mallards alight in the short marsh grass and when I fired at least five hundred greenheads, yellow-nibs, and pintails rose in a brown cloud.

Crouched behind the salt mounds, we had splendid shooting and then rode on to join the carts, our ponies loaded with ducks and geese. The road swung about to the north, and we saw geese in tens of thousands coming into the lake across the mountain passes from their summer breeding grounds in Mongolia and far Siberia. Regiment after regiment swept past, circled away to the west, and dropped into the water as though at the command of a field marshal.

Although we were following the main road to Kwei-hua-cheng, a city of considerable importance not far from the mountains which contained the sheep, we had no intention of going there. Neither did we wish to pass through any place where there might be soldiers, so on the last day's march we left the highway and followed an unimportant trail to the tiny village of Wu-shi-tu, which nestles against the mountain's base. Here we made our camp in a Chinese house and obtained two Mongol hunters. We had hoped to live in tents, but there was not a stick of wood for fuel. The natives burn either coal or grass and twigs, but these would not keep us warm in an open camp.

About the village rose a chaotic mass of saw-toothed mountains cut, to the east, by a stupendous gorge. We stood silent with awe, when we first climbed a winding, white trail to the summit of the mountain and gazed into the abysmal depths. My eye followed an eagle which floated across the chasm to its perch on a projecting crag; thence down the sheer face of the cliff a thousand feet to the stream which has carved this colossal cañon from the living rock. Like a shining silver tracing it twisted and turned, foaming over rocks and running in smooth, green sheets between vertical walls of granite. To the north we looked across at a splendid panorama of saw-toothed peaks and ragged pinnacles tinted with delicate shades of pink and lavender. Beneath our feet were slabs of pure white marble and great blocks of greenish feldspar. Among the peaces were deep ravines and, farther to the east, rolling uplands carpeted with grass. There the sheep are found.

We killed only one goral and a roebuck during the first two days, for a violent gale made hunting well-nigh impossible. On the third morning the sun rose in a sky as blue as the waters of a tropic sea, and not a breath of air stirred the silver poplar leaves as we crossed the rocky stream bed to the base of the mountains north of camp. Fifteen hundred feet above us towered a ragged granite ridge which must be crossed ere we could gain entrance to the grassy valleys beyond the barrier.

We had toiled halfway up the slope, when my hunter sank into the grass, pointed upward, and whispered, "*Pan-yang*" (wild sheep). There, on the very summit of the highest pinnacle, stood a magnificent ram silhouetted against the sky. It was a stage introduction to the greatest game animal in all the world.

Motionless, as though sculptured from the living granite, it gazed across the valley toward the village whence we had come. Through my glasses I could see every detail of its splendid body—the wash of gray with which many winters had tinged its neck and flanks, the finely drawn legs, and the massive horns curling about a head as proudly held as that of a Roman warrior. He stood like a statue for half an hour, while we crouched motionless in the trail below; then he turned deliberately and disappeared.

When we reached the summit of the ridge the ram was nowhere to be seen, but we found his tracks on a path leading down a knifelike outcrop to the bottom of another valley. I felt sure that he would turn eastward toward the grassy uplands, but Na-mon-gin, my Mongol hunter, pointed north to a sea of ragged mountains. We groaned as we looked at those towering peaks; moreover, it seemed hopeless to hunt for a single animal in that chaos of ravines and cañons.

We had already learned, however, that the Mongol knew almost as much about what a sheep would do as did the animal itself. It was positively uncanny. Perhaps we would see a herd of sheep half a mile away. The old fellow would seat himself, nonchalantly fill his pipe and puff contentedly, now and then glancing at the animals. In a few moments he would announce what was about to happen, and he was seldom wrong.

Therefore, when he descended to the bottom of the valley we accepted his dictum without a protest. At the creek bed Harry and his young hunter left us to follow a deep ravine which led upward a little to the left, while Na-mon-gin and I climbed to the crest by way of a precipitous ridge.

Not fifteen minutes after we parted, Harry's rifle banged three times in quick succession, the reports rolling out from the gorge in majestic waves of sound. A moment later the old Mongol saw three sheep silhouetted for an instant against the sky as they scrambled across the ridge. Then a voice floated faintly up to me from out the cañon.

"I've got a f-i-n-e r-a-m," it said, "a b-e-a-u-t-y," and even at that distance I could hear its happy ring.

"Good for Harry," I thought. "He certainly deserved it after his work of last night;" for on the way home his hunter had seen an enormous ram climbing a mountain side and they had followed it to the summit only to lose its trail in the gathering darkness. Harry had stumbled into camp, half dead with fatigue, but with his enthusiasm undiminished.

When Na-mon-gin and I had reached the highest peak and found a trail which led along the mountain side just below the crest, we kept steadily on, now and then stopping to scan the grassy ravines and valleys which radiated from the ridge like the ribs of a giant fan. At half past eleven, as we rounded a rocky shoulder, I saw four sheep feeding in the bottom of a gorge far below us.

Quite unconscious of our presence, they worked out of the ravine across a low spur and into a deep gorge where the grass still showed a tinge of green. As the last one disappeared, we dashed down the slope and came up just above the sheep. With my glasses I could see that the leader carried a fair pair of horns, but that the other three rams were small, as *argali* go.

Lying flat, I pushed my rifle over the crest and aimed at the biggest ram. Three or four tiny grass stems were directly in my line of sight, and fearing that they might deflect my bullet, I drew back and shifted my position a few feet to the right.

One of the sheep must have seen the movement, although we were directly above them, and instantly all were off. In four jumps they had disappeared around a bowlder, giving me time for only a hurried shot at the last one's white rump-patch. The bullet struck a few inches behind the ram, and the valley was empty.

Looking down where they had been so quietly feeding only a few moments before, I called myself all known varieties of a fool. I felt very bad indeed that I had bungled hopelessly my first chance at an *argali*. But the sympathetic old hunter patted me on the shoulder and said in Chinese, "Never mind. They were small ones anyway—not worth having." They were very much worth having to me, however, and all the light seemed to have gone out of the world. We smoked a cigarette, but there was no consolation in that, and I followed the hunter around the peak with a heart as heavy as lead.

Half an hour later we sat down for a look around. I studied every ridge and gully with my glasses without seeing a sign of life. The four sheep had disappeared as completely as though one of the yawning ravines had swallowed them up; the great valley bathed in golden sunlight was deserted and as silent as the tomb.

I was just tearing the wrapper from a piece of chocolate when the hunter touched me on the arm and said quietly, "*Pan-yang li la*" (A sheep has come). He pointed far down a ridge running out at a right angle to the one on which we were sitting, but I could see nothing. Then I scanned every square inch of rock, but still saw no sign of life.

The hunter laughingly whispered, "I can see better than you can even with your foreign eyes. He is standing in that trail—he may come right up to us."

I tried again, following the thin, white line as it wound from us along the side of the knifelike ridge. Just where it vanished into space I saw the sheep, a splendid ram, standing like a statue of gray-brown granite and gazing squarely at us. He was fully half a mile away, but the hunter had seen him the instant he appeared. Without my glasses the animal was merely a blur to me, but the marvelous eyes of the Mongol could detect its every movement.

"It is the same one we saw this morning," he said. "I was sure we would find him over here. He has very big horns—much better than those others."

That was quite true; but the others had given me a shot and this ram, splendid as he was, seemed as unobtainable as the stars. For an hour we watched him. Sometimes he would turn about to look across the ravines on either side and once he came a dozen feet toward us along the path. The hunter smoked quietly, now and then looking through my glasses. "After a while he will go to sleep," he said, "then we can shoot him."

I must confess that I had but little hope. The ram seemed too splendid and much, much too far away. But I could feast my eyes on his magnificent head and almost count the rings on his curling horns.

A flock of red-legged partridges sailed across from the opposite ridge, uttering their rapid-fire call and alighted almost at our feet. Then each one seemed to melt into the mountain side, vanishing like magic among the grass and stones. I wondered mildly why they had concealed themselves so suddenly, but a moment later there sounded a subdued whir, like the motor of an aëroplane far up in the sky. Three shadows drifted over, and I saw three huge black eagles swinging in ever lowering circles about our heads. I knew then that the partridges had sought the protection of our presence from their mortal enemies, the eagles.

When I looked at the sheep again he was lying down squarely in the trail, lazily raising his head now and then to gaze about. The hunter inspected the ram through my glasses and prepared to go. We rolled slowly over the ridge and then hurried around to the projecting spur at the end of which the ram was lying.

The going was very bad indeed. Pieces of crumbled granite were continually slipping under foot, and at times we had to cling like flies to a wall of rock with a sheer drop of hundreds of feet below us. Twice the Mongol cautiously looked over the ridge, but each time shook his head and worked his way a little farther. At last he motioned me to slide up beside him. Pushing my rifle over the rock before me, I raised myself a few inches and saw the massive head and neck of the ram two hundred yards away. His body was behind a rocky shoulder, but he was looking squarely at us and in a second would be off.

I aimed carefully just under his chin, and at the roar of the high-power shell, the ram leaped backward. "You hit him," said the Mongol, but I felt he must be wrong; if the bullet had found the neck he would have dropped like lead.

Never in all my years of hunting have I had a feeling of such intense surprise and self-disgust. I had been certain of the shot and it was impossible to believe that I had missed. A lump rose in my throat and I sat with my head resting on my hands in the uttermost depths of dejection.

And then the impossible happened! Why it happened, I shall never know. A kind Providence must have directed the actions of the sheep, for, as I raised my eyes, I saw again that enormous head and neck appear from behind a rock a hundred yards away; just that head with its circlet of massive horns and the neck—nothing more. Almost in a daze I lifted my rifle, saw the little ivory bead of the front sight center on that gray neck, and touched the trigger. A thousand echoes crashed back upon us. There was a clatter of stones, a confused vision of a ponderous bulk heaving up and back— and all was still. But it was enough for me; there could be no mistake this time. The ram was mine.

The sudden transition from utter dejection to the greatest triumph of a sportsman's life set me wild with joy, I yelled and pounded the old Mongol on the back until he begged for mercy; then I whirled him about in a war dance on the summit of the ridge. I wanted to leap down the rocks where the sheep had disappeared but the hunter held my arm. For ten minutes we sat there waiting to make sure that the ram would not dash away while we were out of sight in the ravine below. But I knew in my heart that it was all unnecessary. My bullet had gone where I wanted it to go and that was quite enough. No sheep that ever walked could live with a Mannlicher ball squarely in its neck.

When we finally descended, the animal lay halfway down the slope, feebly kicking. What a huge brute he was, and what a glorious head! I had never dreamed that an *argali* could be so splendid. His horns were perfect, and my hands could not meet around them at the base.

Then, of course, I wanted to know what had happened at my first shot. The evidence was there upon his face. My bullet had gone an inch high, struck him in the corner of the mouth, and emerged from his right cheek. It must have been a painful wound, and I shall never cease to wonder what strange impulse brought him back after he had been so badly stung. The second ball had been centered in the neck as though in the bull's-eye of a target.

The skin and head of the sheep made a pack weighing nearly one hundred pounds, and the old Mongol groaned as he looked up at the mountain barriers which separated us from camp. On the summit of the first ridge we found the trail over which we had passed in the morning. Half an hour later the hunter jerked me violently behind a ledge of rock. "*Pan-yang*" he whispered, "there, on the mountain side. Can't you see him?" I could not, and he tried to point to it with my rifle. Just at that instant what I had supposed to be a brown rock came to life in a whirl of dust and vanished into the ravine below.

We waited breathlessly for perhaps a minute—it seemed hours—then the head and shoulders of a sheep appeared from behind a bowlder. I aimed low and fired, and the animal crumpled in its tracks. A second later two rams and a ewe dashed from the same spot and stopped upon the hillside less than a hundred yards away. Instinctively I sighted on the largest but dropped my rifle without touching the trigger. The sheep was small, and even if we did need him for the group we could not carry his head and skin to camp that night. The wolves would surely have found his carcass before dawn, and it would have been a useless waste of life.

The one I had killed was a fine young ram. With the skin, head, and parts of the meat packed upon my shoulders we started homeward at six o'clock. Our only exit lay down the river bed in the bottom of a great cañon, for in the darkness it would have been dangerous to follow the trail along the cliffs. In half an hour it was black night in the gorge. The vertical walls of rock shut out even the starlight, and we could not see more than a dozen feet ahead.

I shall never forget that walk. After wading the stream twenty-eight times I lost count. I was too cold and tired and had fallen over too many rocks to have it make the slightest difference how many more than twenty-eight times we went into the icy water. The hundred-pound pack upon my back weighed more every hour, but the thought of those two splendid rams was as good as bread and wine.

Harry was considerably worried when we reached camp at eleven o'clock, for in the village there had been much talk of bandits. Even before dinner we measured the rams and found that the horns of the one he had killed exceeded the published records for the species by half an inch in circumference. The horns were forty-seven inches in length, but were broken at the tips; the original length was fifty-one inches; the circumference at the base was twenty inches. Moreover, mine was not far behind in size.

As I snuggled into my fur sleeping bag that night, I realized that it had been the most satisfactory hunting day of my life. The success of the group was assured, with a record ram for the central figure. We had three specimens already, and the others would not be hard to get.

The next morning four soldiers were waiting in the courtyard when we awoke. With many apologies they informed us that they had been sent by the commander of the garrison at Kwei-hua-cheng to ask us to go back with them. The mountains were very dangerous; brigands were swarming in the surrounding country; the commandant was greatly worried for our safety. Therefore, would we be so kind as to break camp at once.

We told them politely, but firmly, that it was impossible for us to comply with their request. We needed the sheep for a great museum in New York, and we could not return without them. As they could see for themselves our passports had been properly viséed by the Foreign Office in Peking, and we were prepared to stay.

The soldiers returned to Kwei-hua-cheng, and the following day we were honored by a visit from the commandant himself. To him we repeated our determination to remain. He evidently realized that we could not be dislodged and suggested a compromise arrangement. He would send soldiers to guard our house and to accompany us while we were hunting. We assented readily, because we knew Chinese soldiers. Of course, the sentinel at the door troubled us not at all, and the ones who were to accompany us were easily disposed of. For the first day's hunt with our guard we selected the roughest part of the mountain, and set such a terrific pace up the almost perpendicular slope that before long they were left far behind. They never bothered us again.

CHAPTER XV
MONGOLIAN *ARGALI*

Although we had seen nearly a dozen sheep where we killed our first three rams, the mountains were deserted when Harry returned the following morning. He hunted faithfully, but did not see even a roebuck; the sheep all had left for other feeding grounds. I remained in camp to superintend the preparation of our specimens.

The next day we had a glorious hunt. By six o'clock we were climbing the winding, white trail west of camp, and for half an hour we stood gazing into the gloomy depths of the stupendous gorge, as yet unlighted by the morning sun. Then we separated, each making toward the grassy uplands by different routes.

Na-mon-gin led me along the summit of a broken ridge, but, evidently, he did not expect to find sheep in the ravines, for he kept straight on, mile after mile, with never a halt for rest. At last we reached a point where the plateau rolled away in grassy waves of brown. We were circling a rounded hill, just below the crest, when, not thirty yards away, three splendid roe deer jumped to their feet and stood as though frozen, gazing at us; then, with a snort, they dashed down the slope and up the other side. They had not yet disappeared, when two other bucks crossed a ridge into the bottom of the draw. It was a sore trial to let them go, but the old hunter had his hand upon my arm and shook his head.

Passing the summit of the hill, we sat down for a look around. Before us, nearly a mile away, three shallow, grass-filled valleys dropped steeply from the rolling meadowland. Almost instantly through my binoculars I caught the moving forms of three sheep in the bottom of the central draw. "*Pan-yang*," I said to the Mongol. "Yes, yes, I see them," he answered. "One has very big horns." He was quite right; for the largest ram carried a splendid head, and the other was by no means small. The third was a tiny ewe. The animals wandered about nibbling at the grass, but did not move out of the valley bottom. After studying them awhile the hunter remarked, "Soon they will go to sleep. We'll wait till then. They would hear or smell us if we went over now."

I ate one of the three pears I had brought for tiffin and smoked a cigarette. The hunter stretched himself out comfortably upon the grass and pulled away at his pipe. It was very pleasant there, for we were protected from the wind, and the sun was delightfully warm. I watched the sheep through the glasses and wondered if I should carry home the splendid ram that night. Finally the little ewe lay down and the others followed her example.

We were just preparing to go when the hunter touched my arm. "*Pan-yang*" he whispered. "There, coming over the hill. Don't move." Sure enough, a sheep was trotting slowly down the hillside in our direction. Why he did not see or smell us, I cannot imagine, for the wind was in his direction. But he came on, passed within one hundred feet, and stopped on the summit of the opposite swell. What a shot! He was so close that I could have counted the rings on his horns—and they were good horns, too, just the size we wanted for the group. But the hunter would not let me shoot. Hi? heart was set upon the big ram peacefully sleeping a mile away.

"A bird in the hand is worth two in the bush" is a motto which I have followed with good success in hunting, and I was loath to let that *argali* go even for the prospect of the big one across the valley. But I had a profound respect for the opinion of my hunter. He usually guessed right, and I had found it safe to follow his advice.

So we watched the sheep walk slowly over the crest of the hill. The Mongol did not tell me then, but he knew that the animal was on his way to join the others, and his silence cost us the big ram. You may wonder how he knew it. I can only answer that what that Mongol did not know about the ways of sheep was not worth learning. He seemed to think as the sheep thought, but, withal, was a most intelligent and delightful companion. His ready sympathy, his keen humor, and his interest in helping me get the finest specimens of the animals I wanted, endeared him to me in a way which only a sportsman can understand. His Shansi dialect and my limited Mandarin made a curious combination of the Chinese language, but we could always piece it out with signs, and we never misunderstood each other on any important matter.

We had many friendly differences of opinion about the

way in which to conduct a stalk, and his childlike glee when he was proved correct was most refreshing. One morning I got the better of him, and for days he could not forget it. We were sitting on a hillside, and with my glasses I picked up a herd of sheep far away on the uplands. "Yes," he said, "one is a very big ram." How he could tell at that distance was a mystery to me, but I did not question his statement for he had proved too often that his range of sight was almost beyond belief.

We started toward the sheep, and after half a mile I looked again. Then I thought I saw a grasscutter, and the animals seemed like donkeys. I said as much but the hunter laughed. "Why, I saw the horns," he said. "One is a big one, a *very* big one." I stopped a second time and made out a native bending over, cutting grass. But I could not convince the Mongol. He disdained my glasses and would not even put them to his eyes. "I don't have to—I *know* they are sheep," he laughed. But I, too, was sure. "Well, we'll see," he said. When we looked again, there could be no mistake; the sheep were donkeys. It was a treat to watch the Mongol's face, and I made much capital of his mistake, for he had so often teased me when I was wrong.

But to return to the sheep across the valley which we were stalking on that sunlit Thursday noon. After the ram had disappeared we made our way slowly around the hilltop, whence he had come, to gain a connecting meadow which would bring us to the ravine where the *argali* were sleeping. On the way I was in a fever of indecision. Ought I to have let that ram go? He was just what we wanted for the group, and something might happen to prevent a shot at the others. It was "a bird in the hand" again, and I had been false to the motto which had so often proved true.

Then the "something" I had feared did happen. We saw a grasscutter with two donkeys emerge from a ravine on the left and strike along the grassy bridge five hundred yards beyond us. If he turned to the right across the upper edge of the meadows, we could whistle for our sheep. Even if he kept straight ahead, possibly they might scent him. The Mongol's face was like a thundercloud. I believe he would have strangled that grasscutter could he have had him in his hands.

But the Fates were kind, and the man with his donkeys kept to the left across the uplands. Even then my Mongol would not hurry. His motto was "Slowly, slowly," and we seemed barely to crawl up the slope of the shallow valley which I hoped still held the sheep.

On the summit of the draw the old hunter motioned me behind him and cautiously raised his head. Then a little farther. Another step and a long look. He stood on tiptoe, and, settling back, quietly motioned me, to move up beside him.

Just then a gust of wind swept across the hilltop and into the ravine. There was a rush of feet, a clatter of sliding rock, and three *argali* dashed into view on the opposite slope. They stopped two hundred yards away. My hunter was frantically whispering, "One more. Don't shoot. Don't shoot." I was at a loss to understand, for I knew there were only three sheep in the draw. The two rams both seemed enormous, and I let drive at the leader. He went down like lead—shot through the shoulders. The two others ran a few yards and stopped again. When I fired, the sheep whirled about but did not fall. I threw in another shell and held the sight well down. The "putt" of a bullet on flesh came distinctly to us, but the ram stood without a motion.

The third shot was too much, and he slumped forward, rolled over, and crashed to the bottom of the ravine. All the time Na-mon-gin was frantically whispering, "Not right. Not right. The big one. The big one." As the second sheep went down I learned the reason. Out from the valley directly below us rushed a huge ram, washed with white on the neck and shoulders and carrying a pair of enormous, curling horns. I was too surprised to move. How could four sheep be there, when I knew there were only three!

Usually I am perfectly cool when shooting and have all my excitement when the work is done, but the unexpected advent of that ram turned on the thrills a bit too soon. I forgot what I had whispered to myself at every shot, "Aim low, aim low. You are shooting down hill." I held squarely on his gray-white shoulder and pulled the trigger. The bullet just grazed his back. He ran a few steps and stopped. Again I fired hurriedly, and the ball missed him by the fraction of an inch. I saw it strike and came to my senses with a jerk; but it was too late, for the rifle was empty. Before I could cram in another shell the sheep was gone.

Na-mon-gin was absolutely disgusted. Even though I had killed two fine rams, he wanted the big one. "But," I said, "where did the fourth sheep come from? I saw only three." He looked at me in amazement. "Didn't you know that the ram which walked by us went over to the others?" he answered. "Any one ought to have known that much."

Well, I hadn't known. Otherwise, I should have held my fire. Right there the Mongol read me a lecture on too much haste. He said I was like every other foreigner—always joy out of the others; and to make matters worse, the magnificent animal stationed himself on the very hillside where we had been sitting when we saw them first and, with the little ewe close beside him, watched us for half an hour.

Na-mon-gin glared at him and shook his fist. "We'll get you to-morrow, you old rabbit," he said; and then to me, "Don't you care. I won't eat till we kill him."

For the next ten minutes the kindly old Mongol devoted himself to bringing a smile to my lips. He told me he knew just where that ram would go; we couldn't have carried in his head anyway; that it would be much better to save him for to-morrow; and that I had killed the other two so beautifully that he was proud of me.

I continued to feel better when I saw the two dead *argali*. They were both fine rams, in perfect condition, with beautiful horns. One of them was the sheep which had walked so close to us; there was no doubt of that, for I had been able to see the details of his "face and figure." Every *argali* has its own special characters which are unmistakable. In the carriage of his head, the curve of his horns, and in coloration, he is as individual as a human being.

While we were examining the sheep, Harry and his hunter appeared upon the rim of the ravine. They brought with them, on a donkey, the skin and head of a fine two-year-old ram which he had killed an hour earlier far beyond us on the uplands. It fitted exactly into our series, and when we had another big ram and two ewes, the group would be complete.

Poor Harry was hobbling along just able to walk. He had strained a tendon in his right leg the previous morning, and had been enduring the most excruciating pain all day. He wanted to stay and help us skin the sheep, but I would not let him. We were a long way from camp, and it would require all his strength to get back at all.

At half-past four we finished with the sheep, and tied the skins and much of the meat on the two donkeys which Harry had commandeered. Our only way home lay down the river bed, for in the darkness we could not follow the trail along the cliffs. By six o'clock it was black night in the gorge.

The donkeys were our only salvation, for by instinct—it couldn't have been sight—they followed the trail along the base of the cliffs. By keeping my hands upon the back of the rearmost animal, and the two Mongols close to me, we got out of the cañon and into the wider valley. When we reached the village I was hungry enough to eat chips, for I had had only three pears since six o'clock in the morning, and it was then nine at night.

Harry, limping into camp just after dark, had met my cousin, Commander Thomas Hutchins, Naval Attaché of the American Legation, and Major Austin Barker of the British Army, whom we had been expecting. They had reached the village about ten o'clock in the morning and spent the afternoon shooting hares near a beautiful temple which Harry had discovered among the hills three miles from camp. The boys had waited dinner for me, and we ate it amid a gale of laughter—we were always laughing during the five days that Tom and Barker were with us.

Harry was out of the hunting the next day because his leg needed a complete rest. I took Tom out with me, while Barker was piloted by an old Mongol who gave promise of being a good hunter. Tom and I climbed the white trail to the summit of the ridge, while Barker turned off to the left to gain the peaks on the other side of the gorge. Na-mon-gin was keen for the big ram which I had missed the day before. He had a very definite impression of just where that sheep was to be found, and he completely ignored the ravines on either side of the trail.

Not half a mile from the summit of the pass, the Mongol stopped and said, "*Pan-yang*—on that ridge across the valley," He looked again and turned to me with a smile. "It is the same ram," he said. "I knew he would be here." Sure enough, when I found the sheep with my glasses, I recognized our old friend. The little ewe was with him, and they had been joined by another ram carrying a circlet of horns, not far short of the big fellow's in size.

For half an hour we watched them while the Mongols smoked. The sheep were standing on the very crest of a ridge across the river, moving a few steps now and then, but never going far from where we first discovered them. My hunter said that soon they would go to sleep, and in less than half an hour they filed down hill into the valley; then we, too, went down, crossed a low ridge, and descended to the river's edge. The climb up the other side was decidedly stiff, and it was nearly an hour before we were peering into the ravine where the sheep had disappeared. They were not there, and the hunter said they had gone either up or down the valley—he could not tell which way.

We went up first, but no sheep. Then we crossed to the ridge where we had first seen the *argali* and cautiously looked over a ledge of rocks. There they were, about three hundred yards below, and on the alert, for they had seen Tom's hunter, who had carelessly exposed himself on the crest of the ridge. Tom fired hurriedly, neglecting to remember that he was shooting down hill, and, consequently, overshot the big ram. They rushed off, two shots of mine falling short at nearly four hundred yards as they disappeared behind a rocky ledge.

My Mongol said that we might intercept them if we hurried, and he led me a merry chase into the bottom of the ravine and up the other side. The sheep were there, but standing in an amphitheater formed by inaccessible cliffs. I advocated going to the ridge above and trying for a shot, but the hunter scoffed at the idea. He said that they would surely scent or hear us long before we could see them.

Tom and his Mongol joined us in a short time, and for an hour we lay in the sunshine waiting for the sheep to compose themselves. It was delightfully warm, and we were perfectly content to remain all the afternoon amid the glorious panorama of encircling peaks.

PLATE XIV

Where the Bighorn sheep are found

A Mongolian roebuck

At last Na-mon-gin prepared to leave. He indicated that
we were to go below and that Tom's hunter was to drive the

sheep toward us. When we reached the river, the Mongol placed Tom behind a rock at the mouth of the amphitheater. He took me halfway up the slope, and we settled ourselves behind two bowlders.

I was breathing hard from the strenuous climb, and the old fellow waited until I was ready to shoot; then he gave a signal, and Tom's hunter appeared at the very summit of the rocky amphitheater. Instantly the sheep were on the move, running directly toward us. They seemed to be as large as elephants, for never before had I been as close to a living *argali*. Just as the animals mounted the crest of a rocky ledge, not more than fifty yards away, Na-mon-gin whistled sharply, and the sheep stopped as though turned to stone.

"Now," he whispered, "shoot." As I brought my rifle to the level it banged in the air. I had been showing the hunters how to use the delicate set-trigger, and had carelessly left it on. The sheep instantly dashed away, but there was only one avenue of escape, and that was down hill past me. My second shot broke the hind leg of the big ram; the third struck him in the abdomen, low down, and he staggered, but kept on. The sheep had reached the bottom of the valley before my fourth bullet broke his neck.

Tom opened fire when the other ram and the ewe appeared at the mouth of the amphitheater, but his rear sight had been loosened in the climb down the cliff, and his shots went wild. It was hard luck, for I was very anxious to have him kill an *argali*.

The abdomen shot would have finished the big ram eventually, and I might have killed the other before it crossed the creek; but experience has taught me that it is best to take no chances with a wounded animal in rough country such as this. I have lost too many specimens by being loath to finish them off when they were badly hit.

My ram was a beauty. His horns were almost equal to those of the record head which Harry had killed on the first day, but one of them was marred by a broken tip. The old warrior must have weathered nearly a score of winters and have had many battles. But his new coat was thick and fine—the most beautiful of any we had seen. As he lay in the bottom of the valley I was impressed again by the enormous size of an *argali's* body. There was an excellent opportunity to compare it with a donkey's, for before we had finished our smoke, a Mongol arrived driving two animals before him. The sheep was about one-third larger than the donkey, and with his tremendous neck and head must have weighed a great deal more.

After the ram had been skinned Tom and I left the men to pack in the meat, skin, and head, while we climbed to the summit of the pass and wandered slowly home in the twilight. Major Barker came in shortly after we reached the village. He was almost done, for his man had taken him into the rough country north of camp. A strenuous day for a man just from the city, but Barker was enthusiastic. Even though he had not killed a ram, he had wounded one in the leg and had counted twenty sheep—more than either Harry or I had seen during the entire time we had been at Wu-shi-tu.

When we awoke at five o'clock in the morning, Tom stretched himself very gingerly and remarked that the only parts of him which weren't sore were his eyelids! Harry was still *hors de combat* with the strained tendon in his leg, and I had the beginning of an attack of influenza. Barker admitted that his joints "creaked" considerably; still, he was full of enthusiasm. We started off together but separated when six miles from camp. He found sheep on the uplands almost at once, but did not get a head. Barker was greatly handicapped by using a special model U. S. Army Springfield rifle, which weighed almost as much as a machine gun, and could not have been less fitted for hunting in rough country. No man ever worked harder for an *argali* than he did, and he deserved the best head in the mountains. By noon I was burning with fever and almost unable to drag myself back to camp. I arrived at four o'clock, just after Tom returned. He had not seen a sheep.

The Major hunted next day, but was unsuccessful, and none of us went to the mountains again, for I had nearly a week in bed, and Harry was only able to hobble about the court. On the 28th of October, Tom and Barker left for Peking. Harry and I were sorry to have them leave us. I have camped with many men in many countries of the world, but with no two who were better field companions. Neither Harry nor I will ever forget the happy days with them.

It was evident that I could not hunt again for at least a week, although I could sit a horse. We had seven sheep, and the group was assured; therefore, we decided to shift camp to the wapiti country, fifty miles away hoping that by the time we reached there, we both would be fit again.

CHAPTER XVI
THE "HORSE-DEER" OF SHANSI

All the morning our carts had humped and rattled over the stones in a somber valley one hundred and fifty *li*[2] from where we had killed the sheep. With every mile the precipitous cliffs pressed in more closely upon us until at last the gorge was blocked by a sheer wall of rock. Our destination was a village named Wu-tai-hai, but there appeared to be no possible place for a village in that narrow cañon.

We were a quarter of a mile from the barrier before we could distinguish a group of mud-walled huts, seemingly plastered against the rock like a collection of swallows' nests. No one but a Chinese would have dreamed of building a house in that desolate place. It was Wu-tai-hai, without a doubt, and Harry and I rode forward to investigate.

At the door of a tiny hut we were met by one of our Chinese taxidermists. He ushered us into the court and, with a wave of his hand, announced, "This is the American Legation." The yard was a mass of straw and mud. From the gaping windows of the house bits of torn paper fluttered in the wind; inside, at one end of the largest room, was a bed platform made of mud; at the other, a fat mother hog with five squirming "piglets" sprawled contentedly on the dirt floor. Six years before Colonel (then Captain) Thomas Holcomb, of the United States Marine Corps, had spent several days at this hut while hunting elk. Therefore, it will be known to Peking Chinese until the end of time as the "American Legation."

An inspection of the remaining houses in the village disclosed no better quarters, so our boys ousted the sow and her family, swept the house, spread the *kang* and floor with clean straw, and pasted fresh paper over the windows. We longed to use our tents, but there was nothing except straw or grass to burn, and cooking would be impossible. The villagers were too poor to buy coal from Kwei-hua-cheng, forty miles away, and there was not a sign of wood on the

---

[2] A *li* equals about one-third of a mile.

bare, brown hills.

At the edge of the *kang,* in these north Shansi houses, there is always a clay stove which supports a huge iron pot. A hand bellows is built into the side of the stove, and by feeding straw or grass with one hand and energetically manipulating the bellows with the other, a fire sufficient for simple cooking is obtained.

Except for a few hours of the day the house is as cold as the yard outside, but the natives mind it not at all. Men and women alike dress in sheepskin coats and padded cotton trousers. They do not expect to remove their clothing when they come indoors, and warmth, except at night, is a nonessential in their scheme of life. A system of flues draws the heat from the cooking fires underneath the *kang,* and the clay bricks retain their temperature for several horn's.

At best the north China natives lead a cheerless existence in winter. The house is not a home. Dark, cold, dirty, it is merely a place in which to eat and sleep. There is no home-making instinct in the Chinese wife, for a centuries' old social system, based on the Confucian ethics, has smothered every thought of the privileges of womanhood. Her place is to cook, sew, and bear children; to reflect only the thoughts of her lord and master—to have none of her own.

Wu-tai-hai was typical of villages of its class in all north China; mud huts, each with a tiny courtyard, built end to end in a corner of the hillside. A few acres of ground in the valley bottom and on the mountain side capable of cultivation yield enough wheat, corn, turnips, cabbages, and potatoes to give the natives food. Their life is one of work with few pleasures, and yet they are content because they know nothing else.

Imagine, then, what it meant when we suddenly injected ourselves into their midst. We had come from a world beyond the mountains—a world of which they had sometimes heard, but which was as unreal to them as that of another planet. Europe and America were merely names. A few had learned from passing soldiers that these strange men in that dim, far land had been fighting among themselves and that China, too, was in some vague way connected with the struggle.

But it had not affected them in their tiny rock-bound village. Their world was encompassed within the valley walls or, in its uttermost limits, extended to Kwei-hua-cheng, forty miles away. They knew, even, that a "fire carriage" running on two rails of steel came regularly to Feng-chen, four days' travel to the east, but few of them had ever seen it. So it was almost as unreal as stories of the war and aëroplanes and automobiles.

All the village gathered at the "American Legation" while we unpacked our carts. They gazed in silent awe at our guns and cameras and sleeping bags, but the trays of specimens brought forth an active response. Here was something that was a part of their own life—something they could understand. Mice and rabbits like these they had seen in their own fields; that weasel was the same kind of animal which sometimes stole their chickens. They pointed to the rocks when they saw a red-legged partridge, and told us there were many there; also pheasants.

Why we wanted the skins they could not understand, of course. I told them that we would take them far away across the ocean to America and put them in a great house as large as that hill across the valley; but they smilingly shook their heads. The ocean meant nothing to them, and as for a house as large as a hill—well, there never could be such a place. They were perfectly sure of that.

We had come to Wu-tai-hai to hunt wapiti—*ma-lu* (horse-deer) the natives call them—and they assured us that we could find them on the mountains behind the village. Only last night, said one of the men, he had seen four standing on the hillside. Two had antlers as long as that stick, but they were no good now—the horns were hard—we should have come in the spring when they were soft. Then each pair was worth $150, at least, and big ones even more. The doctors make wonderful medicine from the horns—only a little of it would cure any disease no matter how bad it was. They themselves could not get the *ma-lu*, for the soldiers had long since taken away all their guns, but they would show us where they were.

It was pleasant to hear all this, for we wanted some of those wapiti very badly, indeed. It is one of the links in the chain of evidence connecting the animals of the Old World and the New—the problem which makes Asia the most fascinating hunting ground of all the earth.

When the early settlers first penetrated the forests of America they found the great deer which the Indians called "wapiti." It was supposed for many years that it inhabited only America, but not long ago similar deer were discovered in China, Manchuria, Korea, Mongolia, Siberia, and Turkestan, where undoubtedly the American species originated. Its white discoverers erroneously named the animal "elk," but as this title properly belongs to the European "moose," sportsmen have adopted the Indian name "wapiti" to avoid confusion. Of course, changed environment developed different "species" in all the animals which migrated from Asia either to Europe or America, but their relationships are very close, indeed.

The particular wapiti which we hoped to get at Wu-tai-hai represented a species almost extinct in China. Because of relentless persecution when the antlers are growing and in the "velvet" and continual cutting of the forests only a few individuals remain in this remote corner of northern Shansi Province. These will soon all be killed, for the railroad is being extended to within a few miles of their last stronghold, and sportsmen will flock to the hills from the treaty ports of China.

Our first hunt was on November first. We left camp by a short cut behind the village and descended to the bowlder-strewn bed of the creek which led into a tremendous gorge. We felt very small and helpless as our eyes traveled up the well-nigh vertical walls to the ragged edge of the chasm a thousand feet above us. The mightiness of it all was vaguely depressing, and it was with a distinct feeling of relief that we saw the cañon widen suddenly into a gigantic amphitheater. In its very center, rising from a ragged granite pedestal, a pinnacle of rock, crowned by a tiny temple, shot into the air. It was three hundred feet, at least, from the stream bed to the summit of the spire—and what a colossal task it must have been to transport the building materials for the temple up the sheer sides of rock! The valley sinners must gain much merit from the danger and effort involved in climbing there to worship.

PLATE XV

The head of the record ram

Map of Mongolia and China showing route of second
Asiatic expedition in broken lines

Farther on we passed two villages and then turned off to the right up a tributary valley. We were anxiously looking for signs of forest, but the only possible cover was in a few ravines where a sparse growth of birch and poplar bushes, not more than six or eight feet high, grew on the north slope. Moreover, we could see that the valley ended in open rolling uplands.Turning to Na-mon-gin, I said, "How much farther are the *ma-lu?*" "Here," he answered. "We have already arrived. They are in the bushes on the mountain side."

Caldwell and I were astounded. The idea of looking for wapiti in such a place seemed too absurd! There was hardly enough cover successfully to conceal a rabbit, to say nothing of an animal as large as a horse. Nevertheless, the hunters assured us that the *ma-lu* were there, and we began to take a new interest in the birch scrub. Almost immediately we saw three roebuck near the rim of one of the ravines, their white rump-patches showing conspicuously as they bobbed about in the thin cover. We could have killed them easily, but the hunters would not let us shoot, for we were after larger game.

A few moments later we separated, Harry keeping on up the main valley, while my hunter and I turned into a patch of brush directly above us. We had not gone fifty yards when there was a crash, a rush of feet, and four wapiti dashed through the bushes. The three cows kept straight on, but the bull stopped just on the crest of the ridge directly behind a thick screen of twigs. My rifle was sighted at the huge body dimly visible through the branches. In a moment I would have touched the trigger, but the hunter caught my arm, whispering frantically, "Don't shoot! Don't shoot!"

Of course I knew it was a long chance, for the bullet almost certainly would have been deflected by the twigs, but those splendid antlers seemed very near and very, very desirable. I lowered my rifle reluctantly, and the bull disappeared over the hill crest whence the cows had gone.

"They'll stop in the next ravine," said the hunter, but when we cautiously peered over the ridge the animals were not there—nor were they in the next. At last we found their trail leading into the grassy uplands; but the possibility of finding wapiti, these animals of the forests, on those treeless slopes seemed too absurd even to consider. Yet, the old Mongol kept straight on across the rolling meadow.

Suddenly, off at the right, Harry's rifle banged three times in quick succession—then an interval, and two more shots. Ten seconds later three wapiti cows showed black against the sky line. They were coming fast and straight toward us. We flattened ourselves in the grass, lying as motionless as two gray bowlders, and a moment later another wapiti appeared behind the cows. As the sun glistened on his branching antlers there was no doubt that he was a bull, and a big one, too.

The cows were headed to pass about two hundred yards above us and behind the hill crest. I could easily have reached the summit where they would have been at my mercy, but lower down the big bull also was coming, and the hunter would not let me move. "Wait, wait," he whispered, "we'll surely get him. Wait, we can't lose him."

"What about that ravine?" I answered. "He'll go into the cover. He will never come across this open hillside. I'm going to shoot."

"No, no, he won't turn there. I am sure he won't." The Mongol was right. The big fellow ran straight toward us until he came to the entrance to the valley. My heart was in my mouth as he stopped for an instant and looked down into the cover. Then, for some strange reason, he turned and came on. Three hundred yards away he halted suddenly, swung about, and looked at the ravine again as if half decided to go back.

He was standing broadside, and at the crash of my rifle we could hear the soft thud of the bullet striking flesh; but without a sign of injury he ran forward and stopped under a swell of ground. I could see just ten inches of his back and the magnificent head. It was a small target at three hundred yards, and I missed him twice. With the greatest care I held the little ivory bead well down on that thin brown line, but the bullet only creased his back. It was no use—I simply could not hit him. Running up the hill a few feet, I had his whole body exposed, and the first shot put him down for good.

With a whoop of joy my old Mongol dashed down the steep slope. I had never seen him excited while we were hunting sheep, but now he was wild with delight. Before he had quieted we saw Harry coming over the hill where the wapiti had first appeared. He told us that he had knocked the bull down at long range and had expected to find him dead until he heard me shooting. We found where his bullet had struck the wapiti in the shoulder, yet the animal was running as though untouched.

I examined the bull with the greatest interest, for it was the first Asiatic wapiti of this species that I had ever seen. Its splendid antlers carried eleven points but they were not as massive in the beam or as sharply bent backward at the tips as are those of the American elk. Because of its richer coloration, however, it was decidedly handsomer than any of the American animals.

But the really extraordinary thing was to find the wapiti there at all. It seemed as incongruous as the first automobile that I saw upon the Gobi Desert, for in every other part of the world the animal is a resident of the parklike openings in the forests. Here not a twig or bush was in sight, only the rolling, grass-covered uplands. Undoubtedly these mountains had been wooded many years ago, and as the trees were cut away, the animals had no alternative except to die or adapt themselves to almost plains conditions. The sparse birch scrub in the ravines still afforded them limited protection during the day, but they could feed only at night. It was a case of rapid adaptation to changed environment such as I have seen nowhere else in all the world.

The wapiti, of course, owed their continued existence to the fact that the Chinese villagers of the valley had no firearms; otherwise, when the growing antlers set a price upon their heads, they would all have been exterminated within a year or two.

CHAPTER XVII
WAPITI, ROEBUCK, AND GORAL

After the first day we left the "American Legation" and moved camp to one of two villages at the upper end of the valley about a mile nearer the hunting grounds. There were only half a dozen huts, but they were somewhat superior to those of Wu-tai-hai, and we were able to make ourselves fairly comfortable. The usual threshing floor of hard clay adjoined each house, and all day we could hear the steady beat, beat, beat, of the flails pounding out the wheat.

The grain was usually freed from chaff by the simple process of throwing it into the air when a brisk wind was blowing, but we saw several hand winnowing machines which were exceedingly ingenious and very effective. The wheat was ground between two circular stones operated by a blindfolded donkey which plodded round and round tied to a shaft. Of course, had the animal been able to see he would not have walked continuously in a circle without giving trouble to his master.

Behind our new house the cliffs rose in sheer walls for hundreds of feet, and red-legged partridges, or chuckars, were always calling from some ledge or bowlder. We could have excellent shooting at almost any hour of the day and often picked up pheasants, bearded partridges, and rabbits in the tiny fields across the stream. Besides the wapiti and roebuck, goral were plentiful on the cliffs and there were a few sheep in the lower valley. Altogether it was a veritable game paradise, but one which I fear will last only a few years longer.

We found that the wapiti were not as easy to kill as the first day's hunt had given us reason to believe. The mountains, separated by deep ravines, were so high and precipitous that if the deer became alarmed and crossed a valley it meant a climb of an hour or more to reach the crest of the new ridge. It was killing work, and we returned to camp every night utterly exhausted.

The concentration of animal life in these scrub-filled gorges was really extraordinary, and I hope that a "game hog" never finds that valley. Probably in no other part of China can one see as many roebuck in a space so limited. It is due, of course, to the unusual conditions. Instead of being scattered over a large area, as is usual in the forest where there is an abundance of cover, the animals are confined to the few ravines in which brush remains. The surrounding open hills isolate them almost as effectively as though they were encircled by water; when driven from one patch of cover they can only run to the next valley.

The facility with which the roebuck and wapiti had adapted themselves to utterly new conditions was a continual marvel to me, and I never lost the feeling of surprise when I saw the animals on the open hillside or running across the rolling, treeless uplands. Had an elephant or a rhinoceros suddenly appeared in place of a deer, it would not have seemed more incongruous.

After we had killed the first wapiti we did not fire a shot for two days, even though roebuck were all about us and we wanted a series for the Museum. This species, *Capreolus bedfordi*, is smaller both in body and in antlers than the one we obtained in Mongolia and differs decidedly in coloration.

On the second hunt I, alone, saw forty-five roebuck, and Harry, who was far to the north of me, counted thirty-one. The third day we were together and put out at least half as many. During that time we saw two wapiti, but did not get a shot at either. Both of us were becoming decidedly tired of passing specimens which we wanted badly and decided to go for roebuck regardless of the possibility of frightening wapiti by the shooting. Na-mon-gin and the other hunters were disgusted with our decision, for they were only interested in the larger game. For the first two drives they worked only half-heartedly, and although seventeen deer were put out of one ravine, they escaped without giving us a shot.

Harry and I held a council of war with the natives and impressed upon them the fact that we were intending to hunt roebuck that day regardless of their personal wishes. They realized that we were not to be dissuaded and prepared to drive the next patch of cover in a really businesslike manner.

Na-mon-gin took me to a position on the edge of a projecting rock to await the natives. As they appeared on the rim of the ravine we saw five roe deer move in the bushes where they had been asleep. Four of them broke back through the line of beaters, but one fine buck came straight toward us. He ran up the slope and crossed a rock-saddle almost beneath me, but I did not fire until he was well away on the opposite hillside; then he plunged forward in his tracks, dead.

Without moving from our position we sent the men over the crest of the mountain to drive the ravines on the other side. The old Mongol and I stretched out upon the rock and smoked for half an hour, while I tried to tell him in my best Chinese—which is very bad—the story of a bear hunt in Alaska. I had just killed the bear, in my narrative, when we saw five roebuck appear on the sky line. They trotted straight toward Harry, and in a moment we heard two shots in quick succession. I knew that meant at least one more deer.

Five minutes later we made out a roebuck rounding the base of the spur on which we sat. It seemed no larger than a brown rabbit at that distance, but the animal was running directly up the bottom of the ravine which we commanded. It was a buck carrying splendid antlers and we watched him come steadily on until he was almost below us.

Na-mon-gin whispered, "Don't shoot until he stops"; but it seemed that the animal would cross the ridge without a pause. He was almost at the summit when he halted for an instant, facing directly away from us. I fired, and the buck leaped backward shot through the neck.

Na-mon-gin was in high good humor, for I had killed two deer with two shots. Harry brought a splendid doe which he had bored neatly through the body as it dashed at full speed across the valley below him. Even the old Mongol had to admit that the wapiti could not have been greatly disturbed by the shooting, and all the men were as pleased as children. There was meat enough for all our boys as well as for the beaters.

Our next day's hunt was for goral on the precipitous cliffs north of camp. Goral belong to a most interesting group of mammals known as the "goat-antelopes" because of the intermediate position which they occupy between the true antelope and the goats. The takin, serow, and goral are the Asiatic members of this sub-family, the *Rupicaprinæ*, which is represented in America by the so-called Rocky Mountain goat and in Europe by the chamois. The goral might be called the Asiatic chamois, for its habits closely resemble those of its European relative.

I had killed twenty-five goral in Yün-nan on the first Asiatic expedition and, therefore, was not particularly keen, from the sporting standpoint, about shooting others. But we did need several specimens, since the north China goral represents a different species, *Nemorhœdus caudatus*; from the one we had obtained in Yün-nan, which is *N. griseus*.

Moreover, Harry was exceedingly anxious to get several of the animals for he had not been very successful with them. He had shot one at Wu-shi-tu, while we were hunting sheep, and after wounding two others at Wu-tai-hai had begun to learn how hard they are to kill.

The thousand-foot climb up the almost perpendicular cliff was one of the most difficult bits of going which we encountered anywhere in the mountains, and I was ready for a rest in the sun when we reached the summit. Although my beaters were not successful in putting out a goral, we heard Harry shoot once away to the right; and half an hour later I saw him through my binoculars accompanied by one of his men who carried a goral on his shoulders.

On the way Harry disturbed a goral which ran down the sheer wall opposite to us at full speed, bouncing from rock to rock as though made of India rubber. It was almost inconceivable that anything except a bird could move along the face of that cliff, and yet the goral ran apparently as easily as though it had been on level ground. I missed it beautifully and the animal disappeared into a cave among the rocks. Although I sent two bullets into the hole, hoping to drive out the beast, it would not move. Two beaters made their way from above to within thirty feet of the hiding place and sent down a shower of dirt and stones, but still there was no sign of action. Then another native climbed up from below at the risk of his life, and just as he gained the ledge which led to the cave the goral leaped out. The Mongol yelled with fright, for the animal nearly shoved him off the rocks and dashed into the bottom of the ravine where it took refuge in another cave.

I would not have taken that thousand-foot climb again for

all the gorals in China, but Harry started down at once. The animal again remained in its cave until a beater was opposite the entrance and then shot out like an arrow almost into Harry's face. He was so startled that he missed it twice.

I decided to abandon goral hunting for that day. Na-mon-gin took me over the summit of the ridge with two beaters and we found roebuck at once. I returned to camp with two bucks and a doe. In the lower valley I met Harry carrying a shotgun and accompanied by a boy strung about with pheasants and chuckars. After losing the goral he had toiled up the mountain again but had found only two roebuck, one of which he shot.

Our second wapiti was killed on November seventh. It was a raw day with an icy wind blowing across the ridges where we lay for half an hour while the beaters bungled a drive for twelve roebuck which had gone into a scrub-filled ravine. The animals eluded us by running across a hilltop which should have been blocked by a native, and I got only one shot at a fox. The report of my rifle disturbed eight wapiti which the beaters discovered as they crossed the uplands in the direction of another patch of cover a mile away.

It was a long, cold walk over the hills against the biting wind, and after driving one ravine unsuccessfully Harry descended to the bottom of a wide valley, while I continued parallel with him on the summit of the ridge. Three roebuck suddenly jumped from a shallow ravine in front of me, and one of them, a splendid buck, stopped behind a bush. It was too great a temptation, so I fired; but the bullet went to pieces in the twigs and never reached its mark. Harry saw the deer go over the hill and ran around the base of a rocky shoulder just in time to intercept three wapiti which my shot had started down the ravine. He dropped behind a bowlder and let a cow and a calf pass within a few yards of him, for he saw the antlers of a bull rocking along just behind a tiny ridge. As the animal came into view he sent a bullet into his shoulder, and a second ball a few inches behind the first. The elk went down but got to his feet again, and Harry put him under for good with a third shot in the hip.

Looking up he saw another bull, alone, emerging from a patch of cover on the summit of the opposite slope four hundred yards away. He fired point-blank, but the range was a bit too long and his bullet kicked up a cloud of snow under the animal's belly.

I was entirely out of the race on the summit of the hill, for the nearest wapiti was fully eight hundred yards away. Harry's bull was somewhat smaller than the first one we had killed, but had an even more beautiful coat.

We were pretty well exhausted from the week's strenuous climbing and spent Sunday resting and looking after the small mammal work which our Chinese taxidermists had been carrying on under my direction.

Monday morning we were on the hunting grounds shortly after sunrise. At the first drive a beautiful buck roe deer ran out of a ravine into the main valley where I was stationed. Suddenly he caught sight of us where we sat under a rock and stopped with head thrown up and one foot raised, I shall never forget the beautiful picture which he made standing there against the background of snow with the sun glancing on his antlers. Before I could shoot he was off at top speed bounding over the bushes parallel to us. My first shot just creased his back, but the second caught him squarely in the shoulder, while he was in mid-air, turning him over in a complete somersault.

A few moments later we saw the two beaters on the hill run toward each other excitedly and felt sure they had seen something besides roebuck. When they reached us they reported that seven wapiti had run out directly between them and over the ridge.

The climb to the top of the mountain was an ordeal. It was the highest ridge on that side of the valley and every time we reached what appeared to be the crest, another and higher summit loomed above us. We followed the tracks of the animals into a series of ravines which ran down on the opposite side of the mountain and tried a drive. It was too large a territory for our four beaters, and the animals escaped unobserved up one of the valleys. Na-mon-gin and I sat on the hillside for an hour in the icy wind. We were both shaking with cold and I doubt if I could have hit a wapiti if it had stopped fifty feet away.

Harry saw a young elk go into a mass of birch scrub in the

bottom of the valley, and when he descended to drive it out, his hunter discovered a huge bull walking slowly up a ravine not two hundred yards from me but under cover of the hill and beyond my sight.

A little before dark we started home by way of a deep ravine which extended out to the main valley. We were talking in a low tone and I was smoking a cigarette—my rifle slung over my shoulder. Suddenly Harry exclaimed, "Great Scott, Roy! There's a *ma-lu*."

On the instant his rifle banged, and I looked up just in time to see a bull wapiti stop on an open slope of the ravine about ninety yards away. Before I had unslung my rifle Harry fired again, but he could not see the notch in his rear sight and both bullets went high.

Through the peep sight in my Mannlicher the animal was perfectly visible, and when I fired, the bull dropped like lead, rolling over and over down the hill. He attempted to get to his feet but was unable to stand, and I put him down for good with a second shot. It all happened so quickly that we could hardly realize that a day of disappointment had ended in success.

On our way back to camp Harry and I decided that this would end our hunt, for we had three fine bulls, and it was evident that only a very few wapiti remained. The species is doomed to early extinction for, with the advent of the railroad, the last stand which the elk have made by means of their extraordinary adaptation to changed conditions will soon become easily accessible to foreign sportsmen. We at least could keep our consciences clear and not hasten the inevitable day by undue slaughter. In western China other species of wapiti are found in greater numbers, but there can be only one end to the persecution to which they are subjected during the season when they are least able to protect themselves.

It is too much to hope that China will make effective game laws before the most interesting and important forms of her wild life have disappeared, but we can do our best to preserve in museums for future generations records of the splendid animals of the present. Not only are they a part of Chinese history, but they belong to all the world, for they furnish some of the evidence from which it is possible to write the fascinating story of those dim, dark ages when man first came upon the earth.

CHAPTER XVIII
WILD PIGS—ANIMAL AND HUMAN

Shansi Province is famous for wild boar among the sportsmen of China. In the central part there are low mountains and deep ravines thickly forested with a scrub growth of pine and oak. The acorns are a favorite food of the pigs, and the pigs are a favorite food of the Chinese—and of foreigners, too, for that matter. No domestic pork that I have ever tasted can excel a young acorn-fed wild pig! Even a full-grown sow is delicious, but beware of an old boar; not only is he tough beyond description, but his flesh is so "strong" that it annoys me even to see it cooked. I tried to eat some boar meat, once upon a time—that is why I feel so deeply about it.

It is useless to hunt wild pig until the leaves are off the trees, for your only hope is to find them feeding on the hillsides in the morning or early evening. Then they will often come into the open or the thin forests, and you can have a fair shot across a ravine or from the summit of a hill. If they are in the brush it is well-nigh impossible to see them at all. A wild boar is very clever at eluding his pursuers, and for his size can carry off more lead and requires more killing than any other animal of which I know. Therefore, you may be sure of a decidedly interesting hunt. On the other hand, an unsuspecting pig is easy to stalk, for his eyesight is not good; his sense of smell is not much better; and he depends largely upon hearing to protect him from enemies.

In Tientsin and Shanghai there are several sportsmen who year after year go to try for record tusks—they are the real authorities on wild boar hunting. My own experience has been limited to perhaps a dozen pigs killed in Korea, Mongolia, Celebes, and various parts of China.

Harry Caldwell and I returned from our bighorn sheep and wapiti hunt on November 19. He was anxious to go with me for wild boar, but business required his presence in Foochow, and Everett Smith, who had been my companion on a trip to the Eastern Tombs the previous spring, volunteered to accompany me. We left on November 28 by the Peking-Hankow Railroad for Ping-ting-cho, arriving the following afternoon at two o'clock. There we obtained donkeys for pack and riding animals. All the traffic in this part of Shansi is by mules or donkeys. As a result the inns are small, with none of the spacious courtyards which we had found in the north of the province. They were not particularly dirty, but the open coal fires which burned in every kitchen sometimes drove us outside for a breath of untainted air. How it is possible for human beings to exist in rooms so filled with coal gas is beyond my knowledge. Of course, death from gas poisoning is not unusual, but I suppose the natives have become somewhat immune to its effects.

Our destination was a tiny village in the mountains about eight miles beyond Ho-shun, a city of considerable size in the very center of the province. Tai-yuan-fu, the capital, at the end of the railway, is a famous place for pigs; but they have been hunted so persistently in recent years that few remain within less than two or three days' journey from the city.

It was a three days' trip from the railroad to Ho-shun, and there was little of interest to distinguish the road from any other in north China. It is always monotonous to travel with pack animals or carts, for they go so slowly that you can make only two or three miles an hour, at best. If there happens to be shooting along the way, as there is in most parts of Shansi, it helps to pass the time. We picked up a few pheasants, some chuckars, and a dozen pigeons, but did not stop to do any real hunting until we entered a wooded valley and established ourselves in a fairly comfortable Chinese hut at the little village of Kao-chia-chuang. On the way in we met a party of Christian Brother missionaries who had been hunting in the vicinity for five days. They had seen ten or twelve pigs and had killed a splendid boar weighing about three hundred and fifty pounds as well as two roebuck.

The mountains near the village had been so thoroughly hunted that there was little chance of finding pigs, but nevertheless we decided to stay for a day or two. I killed a two-year-old roebuck on the first afternoon; and the next morning, while Smith and I were resting on a mountain trail, one of our men saw an enormous wild boar trot across an open ridge and disappear into a heavily forested ravine. I selected a post on a projecting shoulder, while one Chinese went with Smith to pick up the trail of the pig. There were so many avenues of escape open to the boar that I had to remain where it was possible to watch a large expanse of country.

Smith had not yet reached the bottom of the ravine when the native who had remained with me suddenly began to gesticulate wildly and to point to a wooded slope directly in front of us. He hopped about like a man who has suddenly lost his mind and succeeded in keeping in front of me so that I could see nothing but his waving arms and writhing body. Finally seizing him by the collar, I threw him to the ground so violently that he realized his place was behind me. Then I saw the pig running along a narrow trail, silhouetted against the snow which lay thinly on the shaded side of the hill.

He was easily three hundred and fifty yards away and I had little hope of hitting him, but I selected an open patch beyond a bit of cover and fired as he emerged. The boar squealed and plunged forward into the bushes. A moment later he reappeared, zigzagging his way up the slope and only visible through the trees when he crossed a patch of snow. I emptied the magazine of my rifle in a futile bombardment, but the boar crossed the summit and disappeared.

We picked up his bloody trail and for two hours followed it through a tangled mass of scrub and thorns. It seemed certain that we must find him at any moment, for great red blotches stained the snow wherever he stopped to rest. At last the trail led us across an open ridge, and the snow and blood suddenly ceased. We could not follow his footprints in the thick grass and abandoned the chase just before dark.

Two more days of unsuccessful hunting convinced us that the missionaries had driven the pigs to other cover. There was a region twelve miles away to which they might have gone, and we shifted camp to a village named Tziloa a mile or more from the scrub-covered hills which we wished to investigate.

The natives of this part of the country were in no sense hunters. They were farmers who, now that the crops were harvested, had plenty of leisure time and were glad to roam the hills with us. Although their eyesight was remarkable and they were able to see a pig twice as far as we could, they had no conception of stalking the game or of how to hunt it. When we began to shoot, instead of watching the pigs, they were always so anxious to obtain the empty cartridge cases that a wild scramble ensued after every shot. They were like street boys fighting for a penny. It was a serious handicap for successful hunting, and they kept me in such a state of irritation that I never shot so badly in all my life.

We found pigs at Tziloa immediately. The carts went by road to the village, while Smith and I, with two Chinese, crossed the mountains. On the summit of a ridge not far from the village we met eight native hunters. Two of them had ancient muzzle-loading guns but the others only carried staves. Evidently their method of hunting was to surround the pigs and drive them close up to the men with firearms.

We persuaded one of the Chinese, a boy of eighteen, with cross-eyes and a funny, dried-up little face, to accompany us, for our two guides wished to return that night to Kao-chia-chuang. He led us down a spur which projected northward from the main ridge, and in ten minutes we discovered five pigs on the opposite side of a deep ravine. The sun lay warmly on the slope, and the animals were lazily rooting in the oak scrub. They were a happy family—a boar, a sow, and three half-grown piglets.

We slipped quietly among the trees until we were directly opposite to them and not more than two hundred yards away. The boar and the sow had disappeared behind a rocky corner, and the others were slowly following so that the opportunity for a shot would soon be lost. Telling Smith to take the one on the left, I covered another which stood, half facing me. At the roar of my rifle the ravine was filled with wild squeals, and the pig rolled down the hill bringing up against a tree. The boar rushed from behind the rock, and I fired quickly as he stood broadside on. He plunged out of sight, and the gorge was still!

Smith had missed his pig and was very much disgusted. The three Chinese threw themselves down the slope, slipping and rolling over logs and stones, and were up the opposite hill before we reached the bottom of the ravine. They found the pig which I had killed and a blood-splashed trail leading around the hill where the boar had disappeared.

My pig was a splendid male in the rich red-brown coat of adolescence. The bullet had struck him "amid-ships" and shattered the hip on the opposite side. From the blood on the trail we decided that I had shot the big boar through the center of the body about ten inches behind the forelegs.

We had learned by experience how much killing a full-grown pig required, and had no illusions about finding him dead a few yards away, even though both sides of his path were blotched with red at every step. Therefore, while the Chinese followed the trail, Smith and I sprinted across the next ridge into a thickly forested ravine to head off the boar.

We took stations several yards apart, and suddenly I heard Smith's rifle bang six times in quick succession. The Chinese had disturbed the pig from a patch of cover and it had climbed the opposite hill slope in full view of Smith, who apparently had missed it every time. Missing a boar dodging about among the bushes is not such a difficult thing to do, and although poor Smith was too disgusted even to talk about it, I had a good deal of sympathy for him.

We had little hope of getting the animal when we climbed to the summit of the ridge and saw the tangle of brush into which it had disappeared, but nevertheless we followed the trail which was still showing blood. I was in front and was just letting myself down a snow-covered bowlder, when far below me I saw a huge sow and a young pig walking slowly through the trees. I turned quickly, lost my balance, and slipped feet first over the rock into a mass of thorns and scrub. A locomotive could not have made more noise, and I extricated myself just in time to see the two pigs disappear into a grove of pines. I was bleeding from a dozen scratches, but I climbed to the summit of the ridge and dashed forward hoping to cut them off if they crossed below me. They did not appear, and we tried to drive them out from the cover into which they had made their way; but we never saw them again. It was already beginning to grow dark and too late to pick up the trail of the wounded boar, so we had to call it a day and return to the village.

One of our men carried my shotgun and we killed half a dozen pheasants on the way back to camp. The birds had come into the open to feed, and small flocks were scattered along the valley every few hundred yards. We saw about one hundred and fifty in less than an hour, besides a few chuckars.

I have never visited any part of China where pheasants were so plentiful as in this region. Had we been hunting birds we could have killed a hundred or more without the slightest difficulty during the time we were looking for pigs. We could not shoot, however, without the certainty of disturbing big game and, consequently, we only killed pheasants when on the way back to camp. During the day the birds kept well up toward the summits of the ridges and only left the cover in the morning and evening.

Our second hunt was very amusing, as well as successful. We met the same party of Chinese hunters early in the morning, and agreed to divide the meat of all the pigs we killed during the day if they would join forces with us. Among them was a tall, fine-looking young fellow, evidently the leader, who was a real hunter—the only one we found in the entire region. He knew instinctively where the pigs were, what they would do, and how to get them.

He led us without a halt along the summit of the mountain into a ravine and up a long slope to the crest of a knifelike ridge. Then he suddenly dropped in the grass and pointed across a cañon to a bare hillside. Two pigs were there in plain sight—one a very large sow. They were fully three hundred yards away and on the edge of a bushy patch toward which they were feeding slowly. Smith left me to hurry to the bottom of the cañon where he could have a shot at close range if either one went down the hill, while I waited behind a stone. Before he was halfway down the slope the sow moved toward the patch of cover into which the smaller pig had already disappeared. It must be then, if I was to have a shot at all. I fired rather hurriedly and registered a clean miss. Both pigs, instead of staying in the cover where they would have been safe, dashed down the open slope toward the bottom of the cañon. At my first shot all eight of the Chinese had leaped for the empty rifle shell and were rolling about like a pack of dogs after a bone. One of them struck my leg just as I fired the second time and the bullet went into the air; I delivered a broadside of my choicest Chinese oaths and the man drew off. I sent three shots after the fleeing sow, but she disappeared unhurt.

One shell remained in my rifle, and I saw the other pig

running like a scared rabbit in the very bottom of the cañon. It was so far away that I could barely see the animal through my sights, but when I fired it turned a complete somersault and lay still; the bullet had caught it squarely in the head.

Meanwhile, Smith was having a lively time with the old sow. He had swung around a corner of rock just in time to meet the pig coming at full speed from the other side not six yards away. He tried to check himself, slipped, and sat down suddenly but managed to fire once, breaking the animal's left foreleg. It disappeared into the brush with Smith after it.

He began an intermittent bombardment which lasted half an hour. *Bang, bang, bang*—then silence. *Bang, bang, bang*—silence again. I wondered what it all meant and finally ran down the bottom of the valley until I saw Smith opposite to me just under the rim of the ravine. He was tearing madly through the brush not far behind the sow. As the animal appeared for an instant on the summit of a rise he dropped on one knee and fired twice. Then I saw him race over the hill, leaping the bushes like a roebuck. Once he rolled ten feet into a mass of thorn scrub, but he was up again in an instant, hurdling the brush and fallen logs, his eye on the pig.

It was screamingly funny and I was helpless with laughter. "Go it. Smith," I yelled. "Run him down. Catch him in your hands." He had no breath to waste in a reply, for just then he leaped a fallen log and I saw the sow charge him viciously. The animal had been lying under a tree, almost done, but still had life enough to damage Smith badly if it had reached him. As the man landed on his feet, he fired again at the pig which was almost on him. The bullet caught the brute in the shoulder at the base of the neck and rolled it over, but it struggled to its feet and ran uncertainly a few steps; then it dropped in a little gully.

By the time I had begun to climb the hill Smith shouted that the pig might charge again, and I kept my rifle ready, but the animal was "all in." I circled warily and, creeping up from behind, drove my hunting knife into its heart; even then it struggled to get at me before it rolled over dead.

Smith was streaming blood from a score of scratches, and his clothes were in ribbons, but his face was radiant. "I'd have chased the blasted pig clear to Peking," he said. "All my shells are gone, but I wasn't going to let him get away. If I hadn't kept that last cartridge he'd have caught me, surely."

It was fine enthusiasm and, if ever a man deserved his game. Smith deserved that sow. The animal had been shot in half a dozen places; two legs were broken, and at least three of the bullets had reached vital spots. Still the brute kept on. Any one who thinks pigs are easy to kill ought to try the ones in Shansi! The sow weighed well over three hundred pounds, and it required six men to carry the two pigs into camp. We got no more, although we saw two others, but still we felt that the day had not been ill spent. As long as I live I shall never forget Smith's hurdle race after that old sow.

Although I killed two roebuck, the next day I returned to camp with rage in my heart. Smith and I had separated late in the afternoon, and I was hunting with an old Chinese when we discovered three pigs—a huge boar, a sow, and a shote— crossing an open hill. Crawling on my face, I reached a rock not seventy yards from the animals. At the first shot the boar pitched over the bluff into a tangle of thorns, squealing wildly. My second bullet broke the shoulder of the sow, and I had a mad chase through a patch of scrub, but finally lost her.

When I returned to get the big boar I discovered my Chinese squatted on his haunches in the ravine. He blandly informed me that the pig could not be found. I spent the half hour of remaining daylight burrowing in the thorn scrub without success. I learned later that the native had concealed the dead pig under a mass of stones and that during the night he and his confreres had carried it away. Moreover, after we left, they also got the sow which I had wounded. Although at the time I did not suspect the man's perfidy, nevertheless it was apparent that he had not kept his eyes on the boar as I had told him to do; otherwise the pig could not possibly have escaped.

We had one more day of hunting because Smith had obtained two weeks' leave. The next morning dawned dark and cloudy with spurts of hail—just the sort of weather in which animals prefer to stay comfortably snuggled under a bush in the thickest cover. Consequently we saw nothing all day except one roebuck, which I killed. It was running at full speed when I fired, and it disappeared over the crest of a hill without a sign of injury. Smith was waiting on the other side, and I wondered why he did not shoot, until we reached the summit and discovered the deer lying dead in the grass. Smith had seen the buck plunge over the ridge, and just as he was about to fire, it collapsed.

We found that my bullet had completely smashed the heart, yet the animal had run more than one hundred yards. As it fell, one of its antlers had been knocked off and the other was so loose that it dropped in my hand when I lifted the head. This was on December 11. The other bucks which I had killed still wore their antlers, but probably they would all have been shed before Christmas. The growth takes place during the winter, and the velvet is all off the new antlers by the following May.

On the way back to camp we saw a huge boar standing on an open hillside. Smith and I fired hurriedly and both missed a perfectly easy shot. With one of the Chinese I circled the ridge, while Smith took up the animal's trail. We arrived on the edge of a deep ravine just as the boar appeared in the very bottom. I fired as it rushed through the bushes, and the pig squealed but never hesitated. The second shot struck behind it, but at the third it squealed again and dived into a patch of cover. When we reached the spot we found a great pool of blood and bits of entrails—but no pig. A broad red patch led through the snow, and we followed, expecting at every step to find the animal dead. Instead, the track carried us down the hill, up the bottom of a ravine, and onto a hill bare of snow but thickly covered with oak scrub.

While Smith and I circled ahead to intercept the pig, the Chinese followed the trail. It was almost dark when we went back to the men, who announced that the blood had ceased and that they had lost the track. It seemed incredible; but they had so trampled the trail where it left the snow that we could not find it again in the gloom.

Then Smith and I suspected what we eventually found to be true, viz., that the men had discovered the dead pig and had purposely led us astray. We had no proof, however, and they denied the charge so violently that we began to think our suspicions were unfounded.

We had to leave at daylight next morning in order to reach Peking before Smith's leave expired. Two days after we left, one of my friends arrived at Kao-chia-chuang, where we had first hunted, and reported that the Chinese had brought in all four of the pigs which we had wounded. One of them, probably the boar we lost on the last night, was an enormous animal which the natives said weighed more than five hundred pounds. Of course, this could not have been true, but it probably did reach nearly four hundred pounds.

What Smith and I said when we learned that the scoundrels had cheated us would not look well in print. However, it taught us several things about boar hunting which will prove of value in the future. The Chinese can sell wild pig meat for a very high price since it is considered to be a great delicacy. Therefore, if I wound a pig in the future I shall, myself, follow its trail to the bitter end. Moreover, I learned that, to knock over a wild boar and keep him down for good, one needs a heavy rifle. The bullet of my 6.5 mm. Mannlicher, which has proved to be a wonderful killer for anything up to and including sheep, has not weight enough behind it to stop a pig in its tracks. These animals have such wonderful vitality that, even though shot in a vital spot, they can travel an unbelievable distance. Next time I shall carry a rifle especially designed for pigs and thieving Chinese!

CHAPTER XIX
THE GREAT PARK OF THE EASTERN TOMBS

The sunshine of an early spring day was flooding the flower-filled courtyards of Duke Tsai Tse's palace in Peking when Dr. G. D. Wilder, Everett Smith, and I alighted from our car at the huge brass-hound gate. We came by motor instead of rickshaw, for we were on an official visit which had been arranged by the American Minister. We would have suffered much loss of "face" had we come in any lesser vehicle than an automobile, for we were to be received by a "Royal Highness," an Imperial Duke and a man in whose veins flowed the bluest of Manchu blood. Although living in retirement, Duke Tsai Tse is still a powerful and a respected man.

We were ushered through court after court into a large reception hall furnished in semi-foreign style but in excellent taste. A few moments later the duke entered, dressed in a simple gown of dark blue silk. Had I met him casually on the street I should have known he was a "personality." His high-bred features were those of a maker of history, of a man who has faced the ruin of his own ambitions; who has seen his emperor deposed and his dynasty shattered; but who has lost not one whit of his poise or self-esteem. He carried himself with a quiet dignity, and there was a royal courtesy in his greeting which inspired profound respect. Had he been marked for death in the revolution I am sure that he would have received his executioners in the same calm way that he met us in the reception hall. He listened with a courteous interest while we explained the object of our visit. We had come, we told him, to ask permission to collect natural history specimens in the great hunting park at the *Tung Ling*, Eastern Tombs. Here, and at the *Hsi Ling*, or Western Tombs, the Manchu emperors and their royal consorts sleep in splendid mausoleums among the fragrant pines.

The emperors are buried at the lower end of a vast, walled park, more than one hundred miles in length. True to their reverence for the dead, the Chinese conquerors have never touched these sacred spots, and doubtless will never do so. They belong unquestionably to the Manchus, even if their dynasty has been overthrown by force of arms. According to custom, some member of the royal court is always in residence at the Eastern Tombs. This fact Tsai Tse gravely explained, and said that he would commend us in a letter to Duke Chou, who would be glad to grant us the privileges we asked. Then, by touching his teacup to his lips, he indicated that our interview was ended. With the same courtesy he would have shown to a visiting diplomat he ushered us through the courtyards, while at each doorway we begged him to return. Such is the custom in China. That same afternoon a messenger from the duke arrived at my house in Wu Liang Tajen Hutung bearing a letter beautifully written in Chinese characters.

Everett Smith and I left next morning for the Eastern Tombs. We went by train to Tung-cho, twelve miles away, where a *mafu* was waiting with our ponies and a cart for baggage. The way to the *Tung Ling* is a delight, for along it north China country life passes before one in panoramic completeness. For centuries this road has been an imperial highway. I could imagine the gorgeous processions that had passed over it and the pomp and ceremony of the visits of the living emperors to the resting places of the dead.

Most vivid of all was the picture in my mind of the last great funeral only nine years ago. I could see the imperial yellow bier slowly, solemnly, borne over the gray Peking hills. In it lay the dead body of the Dowager Empress, Tz'u-hsi—most dreaded yet most beloved—the greatest empress of the last century, the woman who tasted of life and power through the sweetest joys to their bitter core.

We spent the first night at an inn on the outskirts of a tiny village. It was a clean inn, too—very different from those in south China. The great courtyard was crowded with arriving carts. In the kitchen dozens of tired *mafus* were noisily gulping huge bowls of macaroni, and others, stretched upon the *kang*, had already become mere, shapeless bundles of dirty rags. After dinner Smith and I wandered outside the court. An open-air theater was in full operation a few yards from the inn, and all the village had gathered in the street. But we were of more interest to the audience than the drama itself, and in an instant a score of men and women had surrounded us. They were all good-natured but frankly curious. Finally an old man joined the crowd. "Why," said he, "there are two foreigners!" Immediately the hum of voices ceased, for Age was speaking. "They've got foreign clothes," he exclaimed; "and what funny hats! It is true that foreign hats are much bigger than Chinese caps, and they cost a lot more, too! See that gun the tall one is carrying! He could shoot those pigeons over there as easily as not—all of them with one shot— probably he will in a minute."

The old man continued the lecture until we strolled back to the inn. Undoubtedly he is still discussing us, for there is little to talk about in a Chinese village, except crops and weather and local gossip.

We reached the Eastern Tombs in the late afternoon of the same day. Emerging from a rocky gateway on the summit of a hill, we had the whole panorama of the *Tung Ling* spread out before us. It was like a vast green sea where wave after wave of splendid forests rolled away to the blue haze of distant mountains.

The islands in this forest-ocean were the yellow-roofed tombs, which gave back the sun in a thousand points of golden light. After the monotonous brown of the bare north China hills, the vivid green of the trees was as refreshing as finding an unknown oasis in a sandy desert. To the right was the picturesque village of Ma-lin-yü, the residence of Duke Chou.

From the wide veranda of the charming temple which we were invited to occupy we could look across the brown village to the splendid park and the glistening yellow roofs of the imperial tombs. We found next day that it is a veritable paradise, a spot of exquisite beauty where profound artistic sentiment has been magnificently expressed. Broad, paved avenues, bordered by colossal animals sculptured in snow-white marble, lead through the trees to imposing gates of red and gold. There is, too, a delightful appreciation of climax. As one walks up a spacious avenue, passing through gate after gate, each more magnificent than the last, one is being prepared by this cumulative splendor for the tomb itself. One feels everywhere the dignity of space. There is no smallness, no crowding. One feels the greatness of the people that has done these things: a race that looks at life and death with a vision as broad as the skies themselves.

At the *Tung Ling* Nature has worked hand in hand with man to produce a harmonious whole. Most of the trees about the tombs have been planted, but the work has been cleverly done. There is nothing glaringly artificial, and you feel as though you were in a well-groomed forest where every tree has grown just where, in Nature's scheme of things, it ought to be.

Although the tombs are alike in general plan, they are, at the same time, as individual as were the emperors themselves. Each is a subtle expression of the character of the one who sleeps beneath the yellow roof. The tomb of Ch'ien-Lung, the artist emperor, lies not far away from that of the Empress Dowager. Stately, beautiful in its simplicity, it is an indication of his life and deeds. In striking contrast is the palace built by the Empress for her eternal dwelling. A woman of iron will, holding her place by force and intrigue, a lover of lavish display—she has expressed it all in her gorgeous tomb. The extravagance of its decoration and the wealth of gold and silver seem to declare to all the world her desire to be known even in death as the greatest of the great. It is said that her tomb cost ten million dollars, and I can well believe it. But a hundred years from now, when Ch'ien-Lung's mausoleum, like the painting of an old master, has grown even more beautiful by the touch of age, that of the Empress will be worn and tarnished.

Charmed with the calm, the peace, the exquisite beauty of the spot, we spent a delightful day wandering among the red and gold pavilions. But fascinating as were the tombs, we were really concerned with the "hinterland," the hunting park itself. Sixty miles to the north, but still within the walls, are towering mountains and glorious forests; these were what we had come to see.

All day, behind three tiny donkeys, we followed a tortuous, foaming stream in the bottom of a splendid valley, ever going upward. At night we slept in the open, and next day crossed the mountain into a forest of oak and pine sprinkled with silver birches. Hundreds of wood-cutters passed us on the trail, each carrying a single log upon his back. Before we reached the village of Shing Lung-shan we came into an area of desolation. Thousands of splendid trees were lying in a chaos of charred and blackened trunks. It was the wantonness of it all that depressed and horrified me.

The reason was perfectly apparent. On every bit of open ground Manchu farmers were at work with plow and hoe. The land was being cleared for cultivation, regardless of all else. North China has very little timber—so little, in fact, that one longs passionately to get away from the bare hills. Yet in this forest-paradise the trees were being sacrificed relentlessly simply to obtain a few more acres on which the farmer could grow his crops. If it had to be done—and Heaven knows it need not have been—the trees might have been utilized for timber. Many have been cut, of course, but thousands upon thousands have been burned simply to clear the hillside.

At Shing Lung-shan we met our hunters and continued up the valley for three hours. With every mile there were fewer open spaces; we had come to a region of vast mountains, gloomy valleys, and heavy forests. The scenery was superb! It thrilled me as did the mountains of Yün-nan and the gorges of the Yangtze. Yet all this grandeur is less than one hundred miles from Peking!

On a little ridge between two foaming streams we made our camp in the forest. From the door of the tent we could look over the tops of the trees into the blue distance of the valley; behind us was a wall of forests broken only by the winding corridor of the mountain torrent.

We had come to the *Tung Ling* especially to obtain specimens of the sika deer (*Cervus hortulorum*) and the Reeves's pheasant (*Syrmaticus reevesi*). The former, a noble animal about the size of our Virginia deer in America, has become exceedingly rare in north China. The latter, one of the most beautiful of living birds, is found now in only two localities—near Ichang on the Yangtze River, and at the *Tung Ling*. When the forests of the Eastern Tombs have been cleared this species will be extinct in all north China.

Early in the morning we left with six hunters. Our way led up the bottom of the valley toward a mountain ridge north of camp. As we walked along the trail, suddenly one of the hunters caught me by the arm and whispered, "*Sang-chi*" (wild chicken). There was a whir of wings, a flash of gold—and I registered a clean miss! The bird alighted on the mountain side, and in the bliss of ignorance Smith and I dashed after it. Ten minutes later we were exhausted from the climb and the pheasant had disappeared. We learned soon that it is useless to chase a Reeves's pheasant when it has once been flushed, for it will invariably make for a mountain side, run rapidly to the top, and, once over the summit, fly to another ridge.

On the way home I got my first pheasant, and an hour later put up half a dozen. I should have had two more, but instead of shooting I only stared, fascinated by the beauty of the thing I saw. It was late in the afternoon and the sun was drawing oblique paths of shimmering golden light among the trees. In a clearing near the summit of a wooded shoulder I saw six pheasants feeding and I realized that, by skirting the base of the ridge, I could slip up from behind and force them to fly across the open valley. The stalk progressed according to schedule. When I crossed the ridge there was a whir of wings and six birds shot into the air not thirty feet away. The sun, glancing on their yellow backs and streaming plumes, transformed them into golden balls, each one with a comet-trail of living fire.

The picture was so indescribably beautiful that I watched them sail across the valley with the gun idle in my hands. Not for worlds would I have turned one of those glorious birds into a crumpled mass of flesh and feathers. For centuries the barred tail plumes, which sometimes are six feet long, have been worn by Chinese actors, and the bird is famous in their literature. It will be a real tragedy when this species has passed out of the fauna of north China, as it will do inevitably if the wanton destruction of the *Tung Ling* forests is continued unchecked.

The next afternoon four sika deer gave me a hard chase up and down three mountain ridges. Finally, we located the animals in a deep valley, and I had an opportunity to examine them through my glasses. Much to my disgust I saw that the velvet was not yet off the antlers and that their winter coats were only partly shed. They were valueless as specimens and forthwith I abandoned the hunt. Before leaving Peking I had visited the zoölogical garden to make sure that the captive sika had assumed their summer dress and antlers. But at the *Tung Ling*, spring had not yet arrived, and the animals were late in losing their winter hair.

In summer the sika is the most beautiful of all deer. Its bright red body, spotted with white, is, when seen among the green leaves of the forest, one of the loveliest things in nature. We wished to obtain a group of these splendid animals for the new Hall of Asiatic Life in the American Museum of Natural History, but the specimens had to be in perfect summer dress.

My hunter was disgusted beyond expression when I refused to shoot the deer. The antlers of the sika when in the velvet are of greater value to the natives than those of any other species. A good pair of horns in full velvet sometimes sells for as much as $450. The growing antlers are called *shueh-chiao* (blood horns) by the Chinese, who consider them of the highest efficacy as a remedy for certain diseases. Therefore, the animals are persecuted relentlessly and very few remain even in the *Tung Ling*.

The antlers of the wapiti are also of great value to the native druggists, but strangely enough they care little for those of the moose and the roebuck. Hundreds of thousand of deerhorns are sent from the interior provinces of China to be sold in the large cities, and the complete extermination of certain species is only a matter of a few decades. Moreover, the female elk, just before the calving season, receive unmerciful persecution, for it is believed that the unborn fawns have great medicinal properties.

Since the roebuck at the *Tung Ling* were in the same condition as the sika, they were useless for our purposes. The goral, however, which live high up on the rocky peaks, had not begun to shed their hair, and they gave us good shooting. One beautiful morning Smith killed a splendid ram just above our camp. We had often looked at a ragged, granite outcrop, sparsely covered with spruce and pine trees, which towered a thousand feet above us. We were sure there must be goral somewhere on the ridge, and the hunters told us that they had sometimes killed them there. It was a stiff climb, and we were glad to rest when we reached the summit. The old hunter placed Smith opposite an almost perpendicular face of rock and stationed me beyond him on the other side. Three beaters had climbed the mountain a mile below us and were driving up the ridge.

For half an hour I lay stretched out in the sun luxuriating in the warmth and breathing in the fragrant odor of the pines. While I was lazily watching a Chinese green woodpecker searching for grubs in a tree near by, there came the faintest sound of a loosened pebble on the cliff above my head. Instantly I was alert and tense. A second later Smith's rifle banged once. Then all was still.

In a few moments he shouted to me that he had fired at a big goral, but that it had disappeared behind the ridge and he was afraid' it had not been hit. The old hunter, however, had seen the animal scramble into a tiny grove of pine trees. As it had not emerged, I was sure the goral was wounded, and when the men climbed up the cliff they found it dead, bored neatly through the center of the chest.

Gorals, sika, and roebuck are by no means the only big game animals in the *Tung Ling*. Bears and leopards are not uncommon, and occasionally a tiger is killed by the natives. Among other species is a huge flying squirrel, nearly three feet long, badgers, and chipmunks, a beautiful squirrel with tufted ears which is almost black in summer and now is very rare, and dozens of small animals. But perhaps most interesting of all the creatures of these noble forests are the only wild monkeys to be found in northeastern China.

The birds are remarkable in variety and numbers. Besides the Reeves's pheasant, of which I have spoken, there are two other species of this most beautiful family. One, the common ring-necked pheasant, is very abundant; the other is the rare Pucrasia, a gray bird with a dark-red breast, and a yellow striped head surmounted by a conspicuous crest. It is purely a mountain form requiring a mixed forest of pine and oak and, although more widely distributed than the Reeves's pheasant, it occurs in comparatively few localities of north China.

One morning as Smith and I were coming back from hunting we saw our three boys perched upon a ledge above the stream peering into the water. They called to us, "Would you like some fish?" "Of course," we answered, "but how can you get them?"

In a second they had slipped from the rock and were stripping off their clothes. Then one went to the shallows at the lower end of the pool and began to beat the surface with a leafy branch, while the other two crouched on the bowlders in midstream. Suddenly, one of the boys plunged his head and arms into the water and emerged with a beautiful speckled trout clutched tightly in both hands. He had seen the fish swim beneath the rock where it was cornered and had caught it before it could escape.

For an hour the two boys sat like kingfishers, absolutely motionless except when they dived into the water. Of course, they often missed; but when we were ready to go home they had eight beautiful trout, several of them weighing as much as two pounds. The stream was full of fish, and we would have given worlds for a rod and flies.

Lü baked a loaf of com bread in his curious little oven made from a Standard Oil tin, and we found a jar of honey in our stores. Brook trout fried in deep bacon fat, regular "southern style" corn bread and honey, apple pie, coffee, and cigarettes—the "hardships of camping in the Orient!"

When we had been in camp a week we awoke one morning to find a heavy cloud of smoke drifting up the valley. Evidently a tremendous fire was raging, and Smith and I set out at once on a tour of investigation. A mile down the valley we saw the whole mountain side ablaze. It was a beautiful sight, I admit, but the destruction of that magnificent forest appalled us. Fortunately, the wind was blowing strongly from the east, and there was no danger that the fire might sweep northward in the direction of our camp. As we emerged into a tiny clearing, occupied by a single log hut, we saw two Chinese sitting on their heels, placidly watching the roaring furnace across the valley.

With a good deal of excitement we asked them how the fire possibly could have originated.

"Oh," said one, "we started it ourselves." "In the name of the five gods why did you do it?" Smith asked. "Well, you see," returned the Chinese, "there was quite a lot of brush here in our clearing and we had to get rid of it. To-day the wind was right, so we set it on fire."

"But don't you see that you have burned up that whole mountain's side, destroyed thousands of trees, and absolutely ruined this end of the valley?"

"Oh, yes, but never mind; it can't be helped," the native answered. Then I exploded. I frankly confess that I cursed that Chinese and all his ancestors; which is the only proper way to curse in China. I assured him that he was an "old rabbit" and that his father and his grandfather and his great-grandfather were rabbits. To tell a man that he is even remotely connected with a rabbit is decidedly uncomplimentary in China.

But when it was all said I had accomplished nothing. The man looked at me in blank amazement as though I had suddenly lost my mind. He had not the faintest idea that burning up that beautiful forest was reprehensible in the slightest degree. To him and all his kind, the only thing worth while was to clear that bit of land in the valley. If every tree on the mountain was destroyed in the process, what difference did it make? It would be done eventually, anyway. Land, whether it be on a hill or in a valley, was made to grow crops and to be cultivated by Chinese farmers.

The wanton destruction which is being wrought at the *Tung Ling* makes me sick at heart. Here is one of the most beautiful spots in all China, within less than one hundred miles of Peking, which is being ruined utterly as fast as ax and fire can do the work. One can travel the length and breadth of the whole Republic and not find elsewhere so much glorious scenery in so small a space. Moreover, it is the last sanctuary of much of north China's wild life. When the forests of the *Tung Ling* are gone, half a dozen species of birds and mammals will become extinct. How much of the original flora of north China exists to-day only in these forests I would not dare say, for I am not a botanist, but it can be hardly less than the fauna of which I know.

If China could but realize before it is too late how priceless a treasure is being hewed and burned to nothingness and take the first step in conservation by making a National Park of the Eastern Tombs!

Politically there are difficulties, it is true. The *Tung Ling*, and all the surroundings, as I have said, belong unquestionably to the Manchus, and they can do as they wish with their own. But it is largely a question of money, and were the Republic to pay the price for the forests and mountains beyond the Tombs it would not be difficult to do the rest. No country on earth ever had a more splendid opportunity to create for the generations of the present and the future a living memorial to its glorious past.

THE END

www.ingramcontent.com/pod-product-compliance
Lightning Source LLC
Chambersburg PA
CBHW022005170726
47994CB00022B/2077

NOCTURNAS

Marcelo Padilla

NOCTURNAS

SEGUNDA EDICIÓN

Mayo 2024

Editado por Aguja Literaria

Noruega 6655, dpto. 132

Las Condes Santiago de Chile

Fono fijo: 56 227896753

EMail: contacto@agujaliteraria.com

www.agujaliteraria.com

Facebook: Aguja Literaria

Instagram @agujaliteraria

ISBN

9789564091211

Nº INSCRIPCIÓN:

2024-A-2848

TAPAS:

Autor Fotografía: Marcelo Padilla

Diseño: Jimena Cortés

ÍNDICE

Prólogo

Mis paredes atesoran las escenas más lujuriosas que muchos hombres desean ocultar en la penumbra. Mis luces iluminan bailes sensuales, así como los más obscenos que mujeres comunes y corrientes puedan ejecutar. En mi pista, bailan; en mi barra, coquetean con los clientes, pero al salir por mi puerta, dejan de actuar, dejan de fingir ser quienes no son. En sus hogares son madres, esposas, hijas. Nadie a su alrededor sospecha de la gran decisión que tuvieron que tomar para estar aquí, buscando salir adelante. Mi música ahoga las fogosas palabras de conquista, así como esos acuerdos y tratos prohibidos; disimula los gemidos y falsos orgasmos. Mis rincones esconden a esposos, abuelos, incluso sacerdotes, quienes, como cualquier otro hombre, buscan disfrutar del placer, la atención, el amor, aunque este último sea falso; aquí es donde lo encuentran. He guardado muchos secretos, y a los verdaderos protagonistas los llevaré conmigo hasta el final de mis días.

Capítulo 1: Otra noche

Otra noche en el club Nocturnas. Son las 19:30, las puertas recién abren, pero ya se respira en el ambiente el aroma a diversión, lujuria y desenfreno. Las luces rojas del club se encienden, iluminando vagamente el interior para dar paso a deseos carnales y prohibidos. A pesar de no tener clientes, apenas unos pocos minutos después de la apertura de puertas, las chicas se impacientan por su llegada. La piden con ansias. Encienden inciensos; otras prenden algo que llaman "palo santo" para atraer fortuna y buena suerte. Algunas se encomiendan a Dios, esperando que la noche sea buena y poder llevarse a casa una buena cantidad de dinero. Al final, ese es el objetivo: el dinero. Los trajes brillantes, las faldas cortas y el maquillaje excesivo atraen a los clientes que van entrando a medida que avanza la noche. Se respira un ambiente de falsa felicidad. Aquí no es el hombre quien se acerca a la chica, sino todo lo contrario.

Con un par de cervezas en la mano derecha y una copa en la izquierda, con el vuelto, Ámbar se dirige a una de las mesas situadas en uno de los rincones, donde convergen los amplios y cómodos sillones rojos. Con un andar firme y sensual, sabe que es su momento. La entrega de los tragos es cuando los clientes observan de pies a cabeza a las chicas. Aprovecha sus tacones para atravesar la pista con gracia, siempre con una sonrisa en el rostro. Debe mantener al menos a uno de ellos concentrado en ella y siendo muy inteligente, sabe que no podrá entretener a los dos. Por eso, les propone llamar a una amiga para que los acompañe. Lanza una mirada y una de sus compañeras se levanta. Mientras camina hacia ellos, Ámbar les pregunta:

—¿Les gusta la chica que viene?

—Se ve muy guapa —responde uno.

—Esperemos que sea tan simpática como tú —agrega el otro.

—Sí, claro, todas aquí somos simpáticas.

—Hola, ¿cómo están? ¿Me puedo sentar? —pregunta Karina.

—Sí, por supuesto que sí.

Conformadas las dos parejas, Karina se levanta enviada por el cliente para comprar un trago para ella. Esta es la dinámica de trabajo en el club: para estar con una de las chicas conversando, debes invitarla a beber un trago. Este es a elección de la chica, pues cualquiera que elija tiene el mismo valor. Se explica esto a los clientes nuevos que ingresan al lugar, para que todo fluya con rapidez y puedan divertirse apenas entran, sintiéndose a gusto. Esta es la principal forma de ganar dinero, mediante la comisión que se les da por la venta de cada vaso o copa.

Un nuevo cliente entra, viene solo. Después del recibimiento y los protocolos de entrada, similares a los que se aplican en cualquier discoteca o bar para adultos, se acerca una de las chicas, Estrella, y le pide un vaso de bebida. Ella, sonriente y coqueta, toma el dinero y se dirige a la ventanilla de pago para pedir la bebida gaseosa. El barman, sonriente, le dice:

—Empezaste con el pie derecho esta noche, Estrella.

Ella le devuelve la sonrisa y le cierra un ojo. En el club saben que, estadísticamente, la mayoría de los hombres que piden solo una gaseosa buscan algo más, algo prohibido que realmente se pasa por alto en el club. Claramente, este no es un prostíbulo, pero en las cabinas privadas de los bailes especiales, se hacen acuerdos extraoficiales entre las chicas y los clientes.

Con confianza y voz sensual, casi desnudando con la mirada, Estrella le entrega el vaso al cliente y le dice:

—¿Me invitarás una copa, cariño, para que nos conozcamos mejor?

El joven, casi por acto reflejo y sin pensarlo, responde:

—Sí, claro.

—¿Cómo te llamas?

—Carlos —responde él, lanzándole una pequeña sonrisa coqueta, como si se tratara de un encuentro casual en un bar cualquiera.

—¿Te vienes a divertir hoy, Carlos, o solo vienes por esa bebida? ¡Aunque no lo creo! —exclama rápidamente Estrella, dejándole entrever que podrían pasar más cosas.

—Esa es la idea, aunque no sé mucho cómo funciona el sistema acá. Es la primera vez que entro a un lugar así. ¿De qué se trata?

—Bueno, Carlos, podemos divertirnos de muchas formas, eso depende de ti. —Siempre con una mirada avasalladora, como una leona que estudia a su presa antes de atacar, poco a poco va penetrando en la curiosidad de él. Se da cuenta de que no tiene experiencia en esos lugares.

—¿Me invitas otra copa? —dice a su cliente, al paso de unos diez minutos.

—¡Claro!

Mientras observa disimuladamente su billetera, se da cuenta de que hay suficiente efectivo para pasar largos ratos con ella y así salvar la noche.

Capítulo 2: Baile privado

Después de pagar las copas, con más confianza, Carlos pregunta:

—¿Qué más podemos hacer aquí?

Estrella responde:

—Tú mandas, mi amor. Aquí podemos hacer lo que quieras. Si quieres, te puedo hacer un baile privado.

—¿Cómo es eso? —pregunta con voz de intriga y una nota de vergüenza.

—Es un baile solo para ti. Pero mejor que lo veas tú mismo. Vale diez mil, y te aseguro que no te arrepentirás —responde con total seguridad en lo que ofrece, con una cuota de picardía en sus ojos, imposible de rechazar.

Toma su mano y lo lleva a una cabina cerrada de un metro por un metro. En su interior, hay una especie de banqueta cuadrada acolchada, más bien un cuadrado forrado completamente de cuero, bastante cómodo. En la parte alta de la pared, cuelga un ventilador que se activa inmediatamente al encender la escasa luz.

— Siéntate aquí, mi amor, mientras voy a pagar el baile.

Sentado allí, Carlos mira a su alrededor y al cielo de la pequeña cabina. Se dice a sí mismo: "¿Dónde estoy metido?", mientras en su rostro se dibuja una sonrisa, tratando de simular los nervios que le invaden.

Por los parlantes suena una canción de Nicky Jam, "La Combi Completa", sinónimo de que alguien ha pagado por un baile privado, ya que esta y otras canciones son las más escuchadas en el club, coincidiendo con una cierta cantidad de minutos para realizarlo.

—Ponte cómodo y disfruta. Puedes tocar todo lo que quieras, siempre y cuando lo hagas con respeto —advierte ella. Se da la vuelta y comienza, moviendo sus caderas y subiendo la falda poco a poco para mostrar con sensualidad su parte trasera.

Sentado, mira fijo su cuerpo, parece hecho a medida. Estira su mano derecha para tocar su trasero, pero ella rápidamente se aparta y toma sus dos manos, obligándolo a acariciarla, a sentir sus pezones. Excitado y extasiado por ese momento, se acerca más, intentando frotar sus partes íntimas en su trasero, hecho a medida, lo hace alucinar con cada roce. Esto la deja saber que él está completamente excitado, listo para dar un paso a lo prohibido. Gira levemente su cabeza y le susurra:

—Llévame a un privado. Llévame, me tienes muy caliente. Allá lo vamos a pasar mejor que aquí. ¿Qué dices? —Mirándolo fijamente, con la excitación plasmada en su rostro.

—Sí, sí —dice Carlos, excitado y dispuesto a todo.

—Si gustas, me pasas la plata del privado y tendrás todo esto para ti solito —le dice, mostrando su parte trasera, que con esa diminuta ropa interior negra la hace ver más voluptuosa, y posa una mano en sus nalgas.

—Hazme tuya —insiste rápidamente, intentando hacer pasar desapercibido el hecho de que, si quiere tener ese cuerpo, tiene que pagar.

—Sí, sí, claro —dice y le entrega el dinero rápido, e intenta olvidar que paga por tener sexo con esta chica desconocida, de la cual nada sabe. La excitación es mucho más fuerte que la cordura, tanto, que ni siquiera pasa por su mente que en casa tiene una mujer que espera y cree que aún está en una reunión con sus compañeros de trabajo. Embobado con la idea de conquistar a esta chica perfecta y sentirse el más afortunado por tenerla atraída, sin esfuerzo.

—Espérame un momento para arreglarme para ti. Voy y vuelvo, ahí te aviso. —Muestra a Carlos el lugar donde se realizará todo.

Mientras, él mira a su alrededor. A esa hora, apenas las 21:15, el recinto está casi lleno. Las chicas se sientan en las piernas de los clientes, algunos con unas copas de más, otros bailan y otros conversan entre ellos, con total normalidad. Algunas de las chicas llevan minifaldas tan cortas que dejan entrever algo más que solo piernas, insinuándose a los clientes para lograr que les paguen un trago o un baile.

—¿Por qué tu copa cuesta tanto si solo estás tomando agua? —se escucha en un rincón del local.

—Lo caro no es el agua, mi amor. Lo caro es mi compañía. Si lo piensas así, no es caro, incluso es barato. Ya, invítame a un privado para pasarla bien —dice Luna a su cliente, al que ha logrado sacar un par de copas con esfuerzo.

—Todavía no —responde, mientras observa a una chica con un short apretado y recortado a mano para mostrar más piel.

Ella se da cuenta de que ese cliente no está dispuesto a pagar más por lo poco que ha logrado. Decide dejarlo y buscar un descanso en el camarín.

El hombre del bigote no es cualquiera, sino un cliente que va a menudo; algunas lo llaman el cura, porque dicen que una de las niñas lo reconoció como tal y afirma que bautizó a su hija hace algunos años, pero nunca nadie se ha atrevido a preguntarle directamente si es verdad que es sacerdote, ya que cuando le gusta una chica no repara en gastos y pide incluso privados con más de una chica; en una ocasión solicitó a tres para que le bailaran al mismo tiempo.

Si la chica no le agrada después de un par de tragos, simplemente la deja ir, tal como lo hizo con Luna en esta ocasión, solo le deja de pagar invitaciones y debe retirarse.

—Oh, Dios mío, ¡qué hombre más cagado! —exclama entrando en el camarín, refiriéndose al cliente de bigote con el cual compartía.

—Te salió tacaño el cura, Lunita —dice Estrella mientras afina los últimos detalles en su vestimenta.

—Sí, apenas me invita unas copas, ojalá invitara a alguna de las chiquillas, porque yo le vi que tenía más plata en la billetera. ¿Y tú? ¿Te vas de luna de miel, Estrella? —dice con tono burlón.

—Sí, mi esposo me está esperando, es muy tímido, pero me pagó dos copas, un baile y un privado, así que la voy a hacer cortita allá adentro para que me siga invitando más copas.

—Qué bien, tienes que aprovechar nomás.

—Sí —responde con una sonrisa—, va a acabar rapidito, porque lo dejé más caliente cuando le hice el baile, yo creo que, si le sigo bailando, ¡acaba ahí mismo! —Suelta una risa burlona.

—Ya, huachita, que te vaya bien allá adentro.

—Gracias, negrita...

Capítulo 3: En el privado

—Ya, corazón, ¡vamos! —dice Estrella a Carlos, indicando que camine hacia un rincón oscuro donde hay otras cabinas un poco más grandes, con luces rojas alrededor, generando un entorno más íntimo y pasional.

El joven mira con nerviosismo mientras cierra la puerta.

—Ya, corazón, hazme todo lo que quieras. Tranquilo, aquí no viene nadie —asegura, mientras le baja el cierre del pantalón.

Tímidamente, comienza a tocarle los pechos y ella, para facilitar la tarea, se baja la blusa blanca semitransparente con dos botones dorados abrochados a la altura de sus senos. Toma su cabeza y la inclina hacia abajo, frotándola en su pecho.

—¡Qué rico, mi amor! Tienes una boca exquisita —empuja aún más hacia abajo, mientras él, sin poner resistencia, baja lentamente hacia su zona pélvica y comienza a besarla. La chica se entrega al placer, olvidando por momentos que ese es su trabajo, disfrutando de lo que este chico con poca experiencia le hace sentir. Para él, es una conquista; quiere hacerla sentir bien, hacerla acabar, como cualquier hombre con su pareja.

En ese momento, se cambia la canción que suena en los parlantes y Estrella vuelve en sí misma. Toma a Carlos del pelo y lo levanta. Ella, con el preservativo en la mano listo para ponérselo, le dice con voz excitada y deseosa:

—Ya, papito, hazme tuya, "házmelo rico" —mientras dice estas palabras, se da la vuelta, levantando su trasero, mostrándolo por completo. Carlos, completamente excitado con los gemidos de placer de ella por el sexo oral, ajusta el preservativo que antes había colocado sin que él se diera cuenta, y entra en ella.

—¡Oh, sí! Qué rico. Dame duro, me gusta así. Me vuelves loca —susurra en su oído, mientras él, extasiado por el placer que le genera la chica de ojos azules, pelo rubio y cuerpo fantástico, llega al clímax. Observa su cola, con una vista perfecta de sus dos grandes nalgas y cierra los ojos casi por instinto, sabiendo que nunca había estado con una mujer tan hermosa.

—Qué rico estuvo, mi amor. Me hiciste acabar, me dejaste loca —dice, tomando sus cosas y una toallita desechable para envolver el preservativo y llevarlo a la basura.

—¿Me vas a esperar, mi amor, para que nos tomemos algo más, o te irás? —pregunta con cara de intriga, pidiéndole con la mirada que se quede.

Satisfecho y entrando en razón de lo que ha ocurrido, mira su teléfono para ver la hora y responde:

—Ah, no sé. Voy al baño y te digo, igual es tarde.

Como quien se despide de su novio, Estrella le dice:

—Bueno, mi amor. Nos vemos entonces —y le da un beso en la cara.

Mientras sale del club, se da cuenta de que en la pista hay una chica bailando en el tubo. Queda deslumbrado ante sus sensuales movimientos. Se marcha pensando en cuál será la próxima excusa para volver a ese lugar que lo ha cautivado y sorprendido por el trato que le dieron. Nunca ha sido abordado de tal forma por una mujer; siempre era él quien con dificultad las buscaba, incluso a su mujer en la cama, no importaba, siempre era él quien tomaba la iniciativa.

En el club Nocturnas, esto es claro. Centrados en las necesidades de los hombres y las cosas que buscan fuera de casa, se forma una atención personalizada para cada cliente. Si quiere dominar la situación, las chicas son sumisas. Si no tiene la personalidad para abordar una situación, es abordado. Si quiere bailar, beber o fumar, eso se hace. La finalidad es satisfacer al cliente, ofreciendo lo que no encuentra en casa. Esa es la idea.

Capítulo 4: Baile de Karina

Así continúa Karina con el espectáculo nocturno, ofreciendo a los clientes un baile en el tubo con gran sensualidad, prescindiendo de trepar en él. Realiza movimientos cargados de erotismo y su mirada penetra a cada hombre con quien entabla miradas. Se mueve alrededor del tubo deslizando sutilmente su mano por él y hacia uno de los clientes, quien la observa fijo, boquiabierto, sin pestañear. Parece no respirar de asombro al ver a esta chica con el pelo ligeramente más abajo de los hombros, las puntas teñidas de rosado para atraer la atención mientras se desplaza por cada rincón. Con apenas un metro cincuenta y cinco, se sitúa sobre Joaquín, un cliente conocido en el local, pero que no ha coincidido previamente con ella. Esta noche, opta por un atuendo más provocativo: medias acanaladas que, debido a su transparencia, dejan ver un diminuto tanga negro debajo, y un peto negro con costuras verde flúor para encender la imaginación de todos. Aunque sin grandes atributos en la parte delantera, se enorgullece de su trasero y lo exhibe a quienes pasan al frente suyo. Con movimientos de caderas sobre Joaquín, lo hace sentir como si estuvieran teniendo relaciones íntimas allí mismo, delante de todos, en aquel sillón rojo iluminado por luces LED que realzan el show ardiente que presenta.

Antes de que transcurran diez segundos, se desplaza rápido para deslizarse por el suelo como si fuera una felina hambrienta. Avanza sigilosa con una mirada penetrante hacia tres amigos que disfrutan del espectáculo, sentados en el sillón de enfrente. A gatas atraviesa la pista y rozando sus labios con la lengua, eleva la temperatura del club. Los clientes vitorean, gritan, aplauden y ríen frotando sus manos. La joven alcanza su destino y, con sus manos, abre las piernas del que está en el centro. Con un movimiento sensual y atrevido, desliza su rostro entre las piernas del cliente, rozando sus partes íntimas con la boca, sin apartar la mirada de sus ojos, y lame sus labios. Todos aplauden y gritan emocionados, algunos incluso corean su nombre, "Karina", lo que a su vez le da más energías a la rubia de puntas rosadas.

En segundos, se sienta encima del joven, le da la espalda, y con movimientos circulares de cadera y la cabeza hacia atrás, comienza a bajar sus manos junto a las suyas. Por su cuello roza lentamente los dedos, deslizándolos hacia abajo con dirección fija, sin hacer pausa alguna, hasta sentir la dureza de su clavícula, como si esta le anunciara el paso hacia sus pechos. Cierra los ojos y, frotando con firmeza las manos del joven en su cuerpo, hace un gesto de excitación, mira hacia arriba y coloca las manos en su entrepierna. Luego, las deja y abre sus brazos para arrastrar sus dedos por los cuerpos de los dos amigos sentados a su lado, mientras avanza el minuto cinco de la canción "Always" de Bon Jovi, preparándose para el gran final de su espectáculo.

Da un brinco para alcanzar el tubo y con destreza ejecuta un giro con la cabeza hacia abajo, deslizándose hasta el suelo en perfecta sincronía con el final de la canción. Todos gritan y aplauden entusiastas por el espectáculo que acaban de presenciar.

Al finalizar su actuación, las chicas regresan a conversar con los clientes que les han invitado alguna bebida, y aquellas a las que no, intentan que les paguen una copa, con el fin de seguir aumentando sus ganancias.

Antes de entrar al camarín, Karina mira a los dos clientes con quienes compartía con Ámbar antes del baile. Les lanza un beso y, al pasar junto a ella, le sonríe y le da un beso en la boca, para provocar a los demás. Le indica que los entretenga mientras se cambia de ropa. Los jóvenes le piden que vaya a buscar tragos para ellos y ellas. Mientras esperan, proponen a Ámbar entrar juntos en un privado, los cuatro al mismo tiempo. Claramente, el beso que vieron les dejó ganas de más, y la fantasía de ver a dos chicas desde un ángulo tan cercano les agita las hormonas, dispuestos a pagar lo que sea.

—¿Qué opinas, Ámbar? —pregunta uno.

—No sé, el espacio no es muy grande y tengo que preguntarle a mi amiga.

—El espacio no importa, donde caben dos caben cuatro. —Ríen ambos jóvenes.

—Pregúntale a tu amiga, porque luego nos iremos.

—De acuerdo, esperen un momento mientras voy por ella.

—Estaremos aquí.

Ámbar se dirige al camarín para ponerse de acuerdo.

—Oye, loca, estos dos quieren hacer un privado los cuatro al mismo tiempo.

—No pensé que sería tan fácil. Los hombres se entusiasman rápidamente con poco.

—Sí, quieren pagar lo que sea, ¿qué te parece?

—Diles que nos compren tragos.

—Ya los compraron. —Ríe.

—Entonces, súmale un baile a cada una, para avisar que ocuparemos una cabina, la más grande.

—Está bien, apúrate.

Ámbar se apresura a cerrar el trato para asegurar una buena venta. Ansiosos, pagan lo que les pide.

—Una fantasía como esta no tiene precio —se dicen, mientras frotan sus manos y mueven los pies, mostrando cierto nerviosismo. Aunque han asistido muchas veces a estos lugares, ambos nunca participaron en una experiencia como esta, por lo que los nervios y la ansiedad son notables, a pesar de sus intentos por disimularlo. Los movimientos de sus cuerpos delatan su estado, aunque el alcohol consigue darles valentía para atreverse.

Desde un rincón, las chicas llaman a los muchachos hacia donde se llevará a cabo dicho encuentro. En ellas también hay algo de nerviosismo, sobre todo en Ámbar, que nunca ha participado en esta experiencia. Se cierra la angosta puerta corrediza detrás de Karina y mira a los chicos que se encuentran parados uno junto al otro, observándolas como dos niños esperando un dulce. Se acerca por el centro de ambos y les dice que se sienten.

—Tenemos veinte minutos para disfrutar, pero primero les tocará mirar, y si gustan, se pueden tocar, se pueden bajar los pantalones, etcétera… —mientras dice esto con voz sensual y respirándole en la nuca a Ámbar, acaricia el rostro de su compañera con la parte externa de su mano, la desliza hacia el cuello, y sigue.

—Yo también quiero mirar —dice Ámbar a los chicos que están embobados, como quien se hipnotiza ante las palabras de un ilusionista.

—Ya… —Es lo único que sale de la boca de uno, mientras comienza a desabrocharse el pantalón.

Ambas se besan con suavidad en los labios, como queriendo conquistarse; es tal la concentración, que la fogosidad que experimentan se transmite a los asistentes.

—Ya, pues, chicos, ¿quién quiere participar? —dice Karina a quienes se frotan con una mano su miembro ante la escena que están presenciando. Se levanta el primero de ellos con una erección que no deja indiferentes a las chicas.

—Me comeré todo eso —dice Karina al joven—, pero primero ponte el preservativo, porque cuando empiece no podré parar.

—Sí… —Asiente con la cabeza.

—Yo igual me lo pondré.

—Será el mejor sexo de mi vida —dice Ámbar mirando al segundo, mientras le pone en la boca el mismo dedo que antes había pasado por la entrepierna de su compañera.

Karina le muerde la oreja al primero y le toma con firmeza el miembro agitándolo, mientras Ámbar le practica sexo oral al otro, intentando hacer que logre llegar a la erección. Se le resbala el preservativo mientras succiona y suelta, pero lo logra afirmar con la mano izquierda que tiene presionando en la parte más baja del pene. Con sus manos le acaricia los testículos, frotándolos entre sí, pero nada funciona.

—¿Qué pasa, hermano? ¿No se te para? —se dirige a su amigo mientras penetra a Karina.

—Cállate que no me puedo concentrar con tus gemidos.

—No me eches la culpa a mí, si a ti no se te para —con tono burlón.

Al parecer los nervios le juegan una mala pasada a Jorge, el segundo chico. Ámbar lanza una mirada a Karina, quien está de espaldas contra la pared, para que le ayude. Posiciona a Jorge frente a Karina, quien sigue siendo penetrada por Sebastián, y como último recurso ambas le practican sexo oral, sin duda es una escena que Jorge no se esperaba, cruza miradas con su amigo y ríen juntos, símbolo de que los nervios están pasando, pero esto no alcanza para lograr una erección.

—Yo también quiero eso —dice Sebastián.

—Y yo también quiero eso que le haces a mi amiga, porque parece que a tu amigo le gusta más mi amiga.

—Cambio de pareja, ¡qué rico! —dice Karina mirando fijo a Jorge.

Ámbar toma la iniciativa con Sebastián y le saca el preservativo en un segundo, al siguiente le pone uno nuevo.

Perplejo, es guiado a sentarse en la banqueta de cuero rojo. Antes de pestañar, ya está encima de él, dando pequeños brincos mientras le jala el cabello. Karina, por su parte, adopta una faceta más sumisa arrodillada ante Jorge, prosigue con el sexo oral. Toma al joven del trasero para empujarlo hacia sí, aprieta sus nalgas y acaricia los alrededores de su ano. Con este último movimiento, siente la dureza en el miembro, como si hubiera actuado por acto reflejo.

—Dame duro, por favor —dice Karina mientras le aprieta fuerte la entrepierna. Se gira rápido desde el suelo y levanta la cola, con la mano izquierda en el suelo, intenta lograr la penetración, ayudada de su mano derecha, pero la erección no es lo suficientemente fuerte, y al paso de los segundos, se empieza a desvanecer.

Los gemidos de placer de Ámbar hacen que Sebastián alcance su clímax, mientras Jorge se da por vencido y se sube el pantalón.

—Oh, qué rico, hermano —dice Sebastián a su amigo.

—Sí, a pesar de que no se me paró nunca, lo pasé bien igual.

—Hazte ver, amigo mío.

—Por tu culpa, si te quejabas más que las chicas.

—No me eches la culpa a mí de que no te funcione el amiguito. —Sonríe.

—Chicos, la pasamos genial, ojalá se repita —dice Ámbar.

—Sí, estuvo agradable igual —agrega Karina.

—Bien, nos iremos a vestir porque el tiempo se ha cumplido, pero si quieren, nos invitan unas copas después…

—Sí, por supuesto —dice Sebastián.

Mientras las chicas se dirigen al camarín para cambiarse, ellos aprovechan para vestirse. Jorge indica a su amigo que ya es hora de retirarse, claramente no haber podido responder en el acto le ha provocado vergüenza y ganas de irse, a lo que su amigo asiente y lo acompaña.

Capítulo 5: Don José

Mientras transcurre la noche, algunos clientes se van y otros llegan, algunos se pasan de copas, tal cual está ahí José, un señor de unos setenta años, con varios tragos de más en el cuerpo, bailando en la pista. Algunos clientes lo miran y ríen, pero claro, José ni cuenta se da, y al parecer, no le importa. Lo que le interesa es pasarlo bien, ya que en casa nadie lo espera y acá se siente acompañado y lo tratan como corresponde.

José es cliente habitual, las chicas lo conocen y lo atienden bien. Sol es la que habitualmente lo hace desde la entrada hasta que lo sube a algún taxi o Uber que lo lleva a su casa. Baila y se ríe junto a él. Luego de un momento, se sienta en el sillón para escuchar sus problemas, prestando atención, ofreciendo algún consejo si así lo pide o una palabra de aliento si se requiere. Después de unos minutos, pasa el dinero a Sol y le dice que vayan a un privado.

—Claro, José, voy y vuelvo. —Caminando hacia el camarín para alistarse, pasa al lado de Rubén.

—Oh, ¡me tiene agotada! —le comenta.

Él se encuentra en una pequeña oficina vigilando las cámaras del local, entre el camarín y el sector de los clientes.

—Sí, pero sabes que don José te hace ganar buena plata.

—Sí, pero eso no quita que me tenga aburrida, contándome las mismas cosas toda la noche. No es tan fácil como crees, hay que estar ahí para saber. Y más encima el olor que tiene, siempre que se le pasan las copas es lo mismo, parece que no termina de orinar y sale del baño porque está pasado a pis.

—Menos mal que en el privado no te hace nada —comenta Rubén, sabiendo que don José solo entra a conversar y que a veces pide a las chicas que bailen para él.

—¡Por lo menos! —exclama Sol con cara de conformidad.

Así, entra junto a José a la pequeña salita que le llaman privado. En esta hay un sillón donde apretaditas caben dos personas, la luz es escasa, pero tiene la privacidad que se necesita. En este caso, para él es el lugar donde puede conversar con más confianza. Aquí también suelta sus lágrimas sin que lo vean, sin que lo cuestionen, sin que se burlen. Viene de una crianza donde no se permite llorar a los hombres, pero aquí encontró un lugar donde nadie lo cuestiona y como dice el lema del club: "Lo que pasa en Nocturnas, se queda en Nocturnas."

Rápidamente transcurren los quince minutos que dura la cita en el privado, pero José no está conforme con esto. Paga por otros quince minutos, pero esta vez le pide a Sol que le baile. Así, da su mayor esfuerzo y complace en todo a su cliente. De manera muy sensual se quita la ropa poco a poco, siempre mirándolo fijo, lo acaricia y se sienta en sus piernas. José pone su mano en la rodilla de la chica y le dice que lo hace muy bonito; pasa la mirada por sus senos y termina en sus ojos. Le toma la mano y se la pone en uno de sus senos.

—Aprovecha de tocarme, José, porque ya sabes que allá afuera no se puede.

El señor de avanzada edad la mira con la boca entreabierta y obedece, moviendo su mano con suavidad alrededor de su pezón. Pasan unos segundos y con la izquierda, que estaba posada en la espalda de la chica, da una palmadita suave en las nalgas.

—Ya, vamos —dice José a Sol para que se levanten y salgan del privado.

—Ya, mi amor, a ver si para la otra me haces más cositas ricas. —A sabiendas de que él nunca le pide sexo.

—Para la otra será. —Se retiran del cuartito.

Capítulo 6: Roxana

A esa hora, en la barra, el cliente de bigote que con dificultad le paga un trago a Luna, está siendo atendido por Roxana, quien sin mucho esfuerzo ha logrado sacarle hartos tragos, cautivándolo con su carita de niña buena, de contextura gruesa, y sin tener tantas curvas, más bien bajita, con espalda ancha, quien, a pesar de tener veinticinco años, demuestra mucho menos. Eso, a algunos clientes les encanta, les excita lo prohibido y esto Roxana lo sabe y saca el máximo provecho. Algunas noches, como esa, se viste con faldita corta tableada, como las que usan las colegialas, más una linda blusa blanca que combina con sus calcetas del mismo color y zapatitos negros. Con la vestimenta ha cumplido la fantasía de muchos hombres; cuando las noches están con poca clientela o cuando no le va muy bien, saca del bolsillo una paleta de dulce, como un mago que revela una carta bajo su manga, e increíblemente un cliente la llama, algunas veces tiene que dar una vuelta alrededor del club comiendo y moviendo el caramelo en su boca, y otras, simplemente se sienta en una silla de la barra a saborear el dulce, lo introduce completamente, luego lo saca y se lo pasa por los labios lentamente. Algunas veces ni siquiera mira a los clientes directo, y eso más llama su atención, imaginan que lo que hace con el caramelo, se lo podría estar haciendo a ellos. Muchos cuentan que es una fantasía que han tenido incluso desde que iban al colegio, miraban a sus compañeras comer el caramelo y se les venían pensamientos sicalípticos inmediatamente, y ahora, tener la posibilidad de llevar a cabo esas fantasías que tantas veces tuvieron, pero nunca pudieron concretar, solo en su imaginación. Una oportunidad así no la pueden dejar pasar, por eso, muchos dicen que lo que imaginaban no se compara con lo vivido, que por cierto se quedaban cortos en sus fantasías. Así Roxana se gana a sus clientes, les ofrece timidez e inocencia en ocasiones, pero con cierto grado de obscenidad para tentarlos a cumplir sus deseos.

Por eso el cliente de bigote le ha pagado tantos tragos, porque le atrae su inocente vestimenta y sabe que podría ir más allá y ser quien le quite la ropa, disfrutar del cuerpo que hay debajo. Pero ella no se lo hace fácil, sabe que la desea, y mucho, pero después de aceptar la invitación para el privado, el hombre queda satisfecho de su deseo y no gasta más.

—Ya pues, linda, vamos a la parte oscura.

—¡Ay, por qué tan rápido!

—Porque quiero subirte esa faldita.

—Oye... ¡qué caliente eres!

—Tú me tienes así, chupando ese dulce.

—Ya, pero primero págame un baile para que sepas a lo que entrarás. —dice con cara picarona.

—Mejor vamos ahora y me bailas allá.

—Ah, entonces no quiero.

—¿Por qué?

—Porque también quiero ver cómo te comportas conmigo, yo no soy como las otras, soy más delicada y me gusta que me traten así.

—¿Y si después te pago el baile y no quieres irte conmigo al privado?

—Fácil, dejemos pagado el baile y me pagas el privado por adelantado, así ya no me puedo negar, y seré tuya de todas formas.

—Ya, listo, ¿cuánto sale todo?

—Ah, y podríamos dejar pagado un traguito para cada uno, porque después del privado seguro necesitaremos hidratación.

—Ya, súmalo a la cuenta total entonces.

—Ya, mi amor, gracias. Te esperaré en la cabina del baile.

Así, Roxana saca el máximo de provecho al cliente que con otras es bastante tacaño, pero ella sabe encontrar la forma de hacerlo gastar. Y de pasada, lograr que otro cliente cumpla sus fantasías sexuales de la adolescencia.

Se acaba la noche y anuncian por los parlantes el final de la jornada, llamando así a las chicas que no están con clientes al camarín, para empezar a desocupar el local, y a los clientes invitándolos a volver en una nueva jornada. Unos salen más rápido que otros, algunos terminan de beber lo que tienen en los vasos mientras comentan las cosas que pasaron en el local, riendo orgullosos y felices de la noche vivida, algunos planificando alguna despedida de soltero o el regalo para algún amigo, sin duda solo buscando la excusa para volver.

Cerradas las puertas y sin clientes en el interior, se encienden las luces, las chicas cambiadas de ropa esperan el Uber que las llevará a casa, comentando algunas experiencias vividas en el turno, o qué tan bien o mal estuvo la noche para cada una. Claro que hay días en que les va bien a todas y otros en que el sacrificio de trabajar allí es más grande que el sueldo que se llevan, pero así es el trabajo en ese rubro y para nada es la "vida fácil", ya que los peligros siempre están, incluso en el camino a casa a altas horas de la madrugada.

Viajando de regreso en Uber, Estrella mira hacia afuera, exhausta por la jornada que acaba de transcurrir. Se reafirma constantemente en que este esfuerzo merece la pena, pues lucha por sus hijos que la esperan. Por ellos se sacrifica y está dispuesta a hacer cualquier cosa por su bienestar. Siendo madre joven y con escasa ayuda, los ha sacado adelante. Este trabajo le ha permitido obtener los recursos necesarios para sostener su salud y continuar con sus estudios. Durante el día le resultaba sumamente complicado conseguir un trabajo debido a la responsabilidad de cuidar al más pequeño. Sin formación universitaria, le costaba mucho encontrar un empleo que cubriera los gastos de la casa, colegios y cuidado infantil. La falta de apoyo y una sólida base familiar dificultaban aún más su situación. Fue entonces cuando encontró en Nocturnas una solución a sus problemas económicos y se comprometió a trabajar durante la noche. Su objetivo primordial es reunir el dinero necesario para adquirir su propia vivienda y brindar una buena vida a sus hijos. Con la esperanza de retirarse de este sacrificado trabajo en el futuro, se motiva a perseverar. Así como ella, otras personas tienen sus razones para encontrarse donde están, todas válidas, difíciles de cuestionar.

Capítulo 7: Jornada de viernes

Hoy es viernes, un día de arduo trabajo en Nocturnas. Muchos vienen después de la jornada laboral a distraerse y divertirse, algunos solos, otros con colegas. Hoy el movimiento en el club comenzará a primera hora. Eso las chicas lo saben, así que llegan puntuales y rápidamente empiezan a maquillarse y ponerse guapas. Eligen los mejores atuendos para iniciar la noche con el pie derecho. Apenas abren las puertas, ingresan los clientes, algunos muy directos, sin duda desean aprovechar al máximo su tiempo y divertirse.

Un grupo de tres amigos pide con rapidez una corrida de cervezas e invitan a tres chicas para que los acompañen. Beben, ríen, conversan al oído, algunos más coquetos que otros, todo con mucha insinuación. Desde un punto de la barra, una chica nueva que llegó a trabajar hoy viernes, mira atentamente. No tiene experiencia en este rubro, así que observa detalladamente los movimientos de sus compañeras.

—Míralas ahí, cómo las chicas coquetean a los tipos esos para que inviten otra copa. ¡Aprende rápido, chica! —dice Perla a Colomba—. Yo también fui nueva, y mira ahora, soy toda una experta en la seducción. —Suelta risitas para aligerar el nerviosismo de la chica nueva.

Perla, venezolana, muy guapa, mide aproximadamente un metro sesenta, tiene caderas anchas, cabello negro que sobrepasa los hombros y piel blanca, muy sensual y carismática. Muchos hombres se enamoran de ella por su *sex appeal* y ternura, y su atractivo visual es innegable. Llegó al club sin experiencia, dejando una vida muy distinta a la que tiene hoy. Era una mujer tranquila dedicada a sus hijos y su hogar, con poca experiencia en la sexualidad, tuvo solo una pareja, el padre de sus hijos, siendo fiel a su marido y su rol de dueña de casa. Sin embargo, esto no fue suficiente para él, por lo que la dejó por otra mujer. Tras irse de su tierra en busca de mejores oportunidades, encontró un lugar donde quedarse, pero los ahorros que tenía no eran suficientes ni serían eternos. Le costó mucho encontrar un trabajo de día. Fue entonces que vio las luces del club encendidas y se armó de valor para entrar a preguntar si podía trabajar ahí. De este modo, comenzó en el rubro de la noche y hoy enseña a Colomba cómo funciona todo en este trabajo.

Avanza la jornada y siguen entrando clientes por diversión. Con la mayor parte de las chicas ocupadas bailando, riendo y animando a los clientes, entran dos y Perla mira a Colomba:

—Ya, nos toca atender.

Ella le responde con cara de nerviosismo.

—Ay, no sé qué tengo que decir.

—Dale, sígueme y saluda a los chicos con un beso en la cara, que aparte están bien guapos. —Con una sonrisa coqueta, cerrando un ojo.

—Hola, muchachos, ¿cómo están? ¿Qué se quieren servir? —comienza Colomba con una mirada tímida y a la vez coqueta.

—Manuel —contesta el cliente, dándole un beso en la cara de inmediato—. ¿Y tú, eres nueva acá? Porque he venido antes y no te he visto.

—Sí, llegué hoy solamente. ¿Y tú, vienes seguido?

—Vine un par de veces —dice con una sonrisa—, pero creo que empezaré a venir más seguido.

—¡Ah, qué bien! Así nos conoceremos más —dice ella con nerviosismo.

—¿Y tú haces bailes privados también?

—No todavía, como te dije, estoy recién llegada y estoy aprendiendo.

—Ah, pero yo te enseño —dice Manuel con actitud seductora y ganas de ser el primero en probar a la nueva.

Pasa el tiempo y, tras un par de tragos, ven que se les hace tarde y no logran concretar sus intenciones. Uno de ellos tiene compromisos familiares que atender, por lo que se despiden y se van.

Capítulo 8: Una clase exprés

—¿Cómo te fue con tu primer cliente? —le pregunta a Colomba.

—¡Bien, creo! Al menos era muy amable y no me presionó para nada.

—¡Woow, tuviste suerte! No siempre pasa así. Normalmente, cuando se dan cuenta de que eres nueva, lo único que quieren es tener sexo contigo para ser los primeros. A mí me pasó eso, pero lo supe aprovechar. Estuve siendo la nueva como una semana porque me pagaban súper bien. Son cosas a las que hay que sacarles provecho —comenta Cleopatra.

—¿Y ya hiciste tu primer baile o aún no?

—No todavía. No sé ni cómo lo voy a hacer.

—Tranquila, tienes que entrar al cuarto del baile y, adentro, tú eres la que manda. Debes mostrar que este es tu lugar de trabajo. Se hace lo que tú dices y dejas que te toquen hasta donde tú quieras. Eso se lo debes dejar súper claro, aunque no te miento, a veces me encantaría que me lo hicieran ahí mismo —dice Cleopatra con risas...

—Mira, ahí viene Fénix.

—¿Quién es?

—El dueño.

—¿En serio?

—Sí, ¿digámosle que te ayude a practicar los bailes privados? Yo entro contigo y te muestro cómo se hacen, ¿te animas?

—Bueno.

Fénix es un hombre de cuarenta, con diez años de experiencia en lo que respecta a la noche. Normalmente intenta pasar desapercibido en el local, es un hombre de bajo perfil, querido y respetado por todos en el club. Cuando llega saluda a todas las chicas libres con un beso, y a las que están ocupadas simplemente les cierra un ojo para saludar, y así no incomodar a los clientes. Saluda y luego entra a la oficina de cámaras o se sienta en el camarín a conversar con alguna de las que está descansando, para saber cómo ha estado la noche y cómo les ha ido. Es su rutina normal.

Hasta este último lugar llega Cleopatra para conversar con Fénix y pedir que la ayude con Colomba para bajar su nerviosismo y, de paso, enseñarle un par de cosas de los bailes privados.

—¿Aún no ha hecho uno?

—No, aún no. No sabe cómo bailarles a los clientes, y quiero mostrarle cómo se hace, pero necesito un modelo —dice con cara coqueta.

—Bueno, será. —A pesar de ser el dueño, no acostumbra a entrar en los bailes con las chicas para evitar comentarios de las demás y mantener la distancia y el respeto.

Se dirigen a una de las cabinas más grandes para entrar los tres.

—Ya, amiga, ahora tienes que mirar todo lo que voy a hacer y decir desde el principio hasta el final, porque bailaré tal cual como se lo hago a los clientes.

—Ya.

—Tienes que pensar que la idea es calentarlos para que después te quieran pagar un privado y así ganar más plata.

Asiente con la cabeza.

—Así que tienes que ser coqueta y calentona, deja la vergüenza a un lado...

Empieza a sonar Ivy Queen en los parlantes con la canción: "Quiero Bailar", y comienza la lección.

—Siéntate, mi amor, y disfruta del baile. Ahora sí puedes tocar, pero por favor no seas brusco para que disfrutes bien del baile.

Cleo empieza su baile frente a Fénix con movimientos lentos, pero muy sensuales. Con mirada fija en sus ojos, quien, acostumbrado a ver bailes, se la devuelve, queriendo intimidarla, como diciéndole: "¿Qué más tienes?". Todo esto bajo el ojo atento de Colomba, que apenas pestañea. Cleo se da la vuelta y le guiña, mostrándole lo que va a hacer, mientras se acerca a él con movimientos sensuales, roza su cuerpo y mueve sus caderas de forma circular.

Él, por acto reflejo, pone sus manos en la cintura de Cleo y ella le lanza una pequeña sonrisa a Colomba, como diciéndole: "Ya lo tengo". Empuja con su trasero hacia atrás realzando los movimientos de cadera. Cleo levanta el brazo derecho y va pasando su mano desde su boca hasta encontrarse con la de su jefe, ahí se la toma y la arrastra hasta su entrepierna, dejándola bien apretada, mientras con la otra le acaricia los genitales por encima del pantalón, siempre con una actitud fogosa y ardiente, mostrándole al cliente que desea tanto que le hagan el amor. Colomba mira con un poco de timidez, ya que esta es la primera vez que ve un baile así desde tan cerca, se siente acalorada ante tanta sensualidad y pasión.

Cleo se da la vuelta, muy pegada al cuerpo de Fénix y con movimientos pélvicos roza los labios por su cuello, mientras pone las manos en el trasero y lo pega aún más a él. Ambos, con movimientos sexuales, se dejan llevar por la pasión. Cleo capta que la canción está a punto de terminar, faltando menos de un minuto. Baja su mano para abrir el pantalón de Fénix y, a la vez, voltea la cabeza mirando a su compañera y le dice:

—Esto se hace con los clientes, y esto es un regalo para el jefe. —Se agacha y, sin preámbulo, le empieza a hacer sexo oral delante de Colomba que la mira ya menos tímida por todo lo experimentado dentro de aquella cabina de 2x2. Mientras mira atenta cómo Cleo se introduce todo el pene de Fénix en la boca y pasa sus manos por su pecho, escucha una voz masculina:

—Ya, Colomba, te toca.

Levanta la mirada y ve cómo el jefe la está mirando fijo, con una pequeña sonrisa en el rostro mientras aún está Cleo agachada. Sin palabras, Colomba queda perpleja pensando: "¿Me toca? ¿Qué me toca? ¿Me está pidiendo que me una a Cleo?".

—Te toca bailar, vamos a ver si aprendiste algo, le dice Fénix a la vez que levanta de un brazo a Cleo y se sube el pantalón.

—Vamos a esperar a que empiece una canción desde el principio. Mientras tanto, haz todas las preguntas a tu compañera para que, cuando bailes, no te distraigas y lo hagas tal como si fuera un cliente. Voy a buscar una cerveza mientras tanto te alistas.

—¿Ya, weona, te gustó el baile?

—Sí, pero no sé si podré hacerlo como tú.

—Tranquila, tienes que dejarte llevar. Primero dile que te trate bien, y luego, imagina que estás sola bailando. Puedes cerrar los ojos para sentirte más sensual. Normalmente, los clientes se te pegan solos. Fénix es la excepción, porque está acostumbrado a esto, por eso le tuve que tomar las manos yo misma. Pero a los demás, hay que estar sacándoselas para que te dejen bailar. Pero piensa que la finalidad es que te paguen un privado, ya que con eso sí que vas a ganar plata.

Capítulo 9: La chica nueva

El jefe entra una vez más al cuarto donde se encuentran las dos chicas conversando. Fénix se da cuenta del aparente nerviosismo de Colomba, así que bromea y cuenta que en el caño hay un hombre mayor bailando, claramente, con copas de más.

—Cleo, te están esperando en la barra, te busca un cliente.

—¡Ah! Ya, jefe, voy entonces. ¡Buena suerte, weona!

—Colomba, relájate. Esto no es una prueba. Yo no soy un cliente, así que esto es simplemente un ensayo para cuando te toque hacer un baile. Mientras, puedes preguntarme lo que quieras o hablar para que te sientas más relajada.

Eso calmó en cierto modo a la chica.

—Bueno, jefe, gracias, pero estoy bien, así que trataré de hacerlo como si fuera un cliente y cuando termine, usted me dice qué tal.

Comienza a sonar la música y, con sensualidad, Colomba se echa hacia atrás con la espalda hacia la pared. Se mueve al ritmo de "Punto G" de Karol G, con la mirada fija en los ojos de aquel hombre que nadie intimida y con mucha confianza en sí misma, como si fuera otra persona. Avanza hacia él con una mano en la cabeza y la otra frotándola con excitación sobre sus senos. Roza apenas con sus labios el cuello del hombre. Lo alcanza con su respiración, logrando que se le erice la piel; con más confianza en sí, se da vuelta y, mientras mueve sus caderas, pone una de las manos de él en su pecho y, al mismo tiempo, baja su sostén, tentando a Fénix a tomar la iniciativa.

Él, con suavidad y tranquilidad, desliza sus dedos hacia abajo para acariciar suavemente los pezones de la chica, uno a la vez. La música, la luz roja y el lugar de apenas 2x2 permiten hacer cosas que nadie más verá, solo las dos personas que están adentro. Por eso es el lugar perfecto para que los clientes se dejen llevar por la lujuria y las chicas logren su objetivo: tentarlos para obtener la máxima ganancia. Porque claro, y eso no deben olvidarlo, ese es su trabajo: la seducción, la entrega de atención, placer o lo que quiera el cliente.

En ese punto del baile, Fénix está bastante excitado. Le cautiva la idea de acariciar, con toda confianza y libertad a la chica nueva y sin experiencia. Sobre todo porque ella se lo pide. Así que mientras acaricia con suavidad el abdomen de Colomba, no se resiste y comienza a besar la parte trasera de su cuello con la clara intención de devolver sus provocaciones. Entonces, baja la mano hacia la entrepierna de la chica, pero a esas alturas, Colomba está tan concentrada en el baile que está más que excitada. Tras las caricias y besos de Fénix, se da vuelta y lo besa en la boca.

—Me gustaría que usted sea el primero en todo, aquí en el club.

Sorprendido y complacido, Fénix se deja llevar por el momento y, con una leve sonrisa en su expresión, le da a entender que está dispuesto a complacer sus deseos. Por si no queda muy claro, con su mano izquierda quita el seguro de su cinturón y lo afloja levemente. La chica besa su cuello y baja, mientras aprieta fuerte con su mano izquierda su miembro, a estas alturas, bastante erecto.

Con confianza, Fénix toma del cabello a la chica, como haciéndole una cola, y la guía para que abra la boca. Ella no solo le practica sexo oral, sino que realmente acaricia el pene con su boca, usando cada parte. A ratos, lo aprieta con la lengua y el paladar, o arrastra sus labios a lo largo. Parece realmente disfrutar lo que está haciendo, incluso cuando él presiona para que llegue más adentro.

—El mejor sexo oral que me han hecho, lejos —dice a Colomba mientras la levanta, con un tono de satisfacción, excitación y deseo de seguir descubriendo más cosas de ella.

—Mentiroso, apuesto que dice lo mismo a todas.

—No necesito mentir, solo digo lo que es. Te hubiera dejado seguir hasta hacerme acabar en tu boca, pero no me quiero quedar con las ganas de probar esto de acá. —Posa su mano derecha en la entrepierna de ella, mientras con la izquierda le baja suavemente el calzoncito diminuto de color negro que trae puesto.

La chica nueva toma el pene de su jefe y lo pone justo en su entrepierna, haciendo rozar ambas partes íntimas.

—¡Ayayai, qué rico! —exclama Fénix, sabiendo lo que se viene.

—Toma, abre el preservativo mientras aseguro la puerta. No quiero que me vaya a ver alguna de las chicas.

—Ah, pero jefe, con usted no necesito usar preservativo. Si yo igual me cuido.

Fénix la mira directo a los ojos y, con una pequeña sonrisa fingida, le dice:

—La lección más importante que vas a aprender aquí es que no importa si la persona con la que tendrás relaciones es bonita, fea, joven, vieja o como sea, tienes que usar preservativo siempre porque tú no puedes saber con quién estuvo esa persona. Y si no quiere usar preservativo contigo, significa que no usa con nadie. Una infección se transmite en segundos, y aparte tienes que aprender a poner el condón tú misma, así te aseguras de que estará ahí para la penetración.

—Bueno, usted manda. Enséñeme cómo se hace. ¿Qué hago primero?

—Primero que todo, si tu cliente está excitado, la idea es que no se le baje la calentura. Mientras abres el sobre del condón, le dices cosas al oído como: "Ya quiero que me la metas, hazme tuya, la tienes muy grande", etcétera.

—¿Y con usted resultan esas frasecitas, jefe?

—A veces. Después de sacar el condón, te agachas. Si te arrodillas, mucho mejor, a los hombres les gusta sentirse superiores. Eso también es un punto de excitación. Todo suma si quieres que acabe rápido y que vuelva por ti. Ya en esa posición, comienzas a deslizar el preservativo en el pene.

Fénix toma el condón y se lo pone en la punta, mostrándole a Colomba cómo. Luego, toma su mano, deslizándola para que el preservativo se acomode. Desliza, lo suelta y lo vuelve a hacer. Eso lo repite hasta que está bien puesto, hasta el final.

—¿Y si no la tienen parada? —pregunta la chica mientras acaricia con una mano los genitales del hombre y, a la vez, le da pequeños besitos en la punta.

—Esa lección te la enseñaré después —contesta Fénix mientras la levanta de un brazo, para comenzar con lo que ha estado esperando.

Le da unos besitos por el cuello, apenas rozando con los labios hasta llegar a su oreja. Se da cuenta de que con esto la joven se excita mucho, y eso lo sabe aprovechar el experimentado jefe, quien siente cómo se le eriza la piel a la muchacha mientras frunce su hermoso y redondo rostro.

Rodea su cintura con un brazo y la levanta. La chica, casi por instinto, abre sus piernas, quedando encajada en las caderas del hombre. Mientras besa sus pechos, usa su mano izquierda para sacar el hilo que poco y nada cubre su trasero. Fénix inicia la penetración con la chica en brazos. Los cincuenta y nueve kilos que pesa parecen no ser nada para él. Después de introducirse en su interior, comienza a mover suavemente su pelvis, haciendo que la penetración sea cada vez más profunda. En tanto, ella empuja su cabeza hacia sus pechos, jalándolo del cabello con una especie de desesperación, producto de la excitación del momento. Nunca lo ha hecho de esa forma, y sentirse casi en el aire le provoca un placer y excitación que jamás ha sentido.

—Ahora viene la mejor parte —dice el hombre a la chica que, a estas alturas, apenas puede escuchar la música.

La excitación de ella es tal que su cabeza solo puede pensar en el suave movimiento adentro y afuera que siente, mezclado con la presión que ejercen sus labios vaginales hacia el miembro que allí adentro se encuentra.

Fénix siente cómo todo allí abajo está totalmente lubricado y comienza a moverse más rápido. Pasa su brazo derecho por debajo de la pierna de la chica y luego hace lo propio con el izquierdo, dejando las piernas de la joven completamente abiertas, dando paso a una penetración más profunda.

Los gemidos en su oído aumentan la excitación y el movimiento adentro y afuera aumenta de velocidad.

Colomba siente que Fénix la va a atravesar. Nunca ha sentido una penetración tan profunda, nunca ha sentido placer de la forma que en ese momento está sintiendo, y piensa: "Pero cómo nunca antes había hecho esta posición.

¿Cómo es posible sentirlo tan adentro? Siento que explotaré de placer".

Muerde su propio antebrazo para evitar subir el volumen de su voz, pero casi no puede contenerse. Mientras Fénix, casi poseído, continúa firme sus movimientos punzantes.

—¡Voy a acabar, ya no puedo más! —exclama en el oído del hombre.

Fénix comienza a besar el cuello a la chica, como si se lo quisiera comer, besando a boca abierta hasta llegar a la clavícula. Y como la llama de una vela que, antes de extinguirse, aumenta su fuego al máximo, el hombre aumenta su potencia. Con la cara enrojecida por el esfuerzo y el cuerpo empapado de sudor, como si hubiera corrido una maratón, le da los últimos empujones para llegar al clímax total y acabar juntos.

Sin duda, hacerlo de forma escondida, tratando de que nadie se diera cuenta, un detonante para aumentar los niveles de excitación. Incluso para Fénix, quien obviamente no se encuentra en esa posición por primera vez, pero nunca ha estado con alguien habiendo público en el local. Eso es nuevo, y lo hace experimentar un orgasmo distinto, como con cada parte de su cuerpo. De hecho, ambos se sienten para tomar un gran respiro y digerir lo que ha pasado.

—Tu baile salió excelente.

—Gracias, si usted lo dice.

—Pon atención a cada cliente. Todos quieren algo diferente o de distinta forma. Así logras leer lo que quieren. Podrás conseguir lo que quieras. Saldré primero, para que te termines de arreglar, luego te preparas para seguir atendiendo, se siente que hay bastantes clientes en el local.

—Sí, claro, como diga. Gracias por todo.

Sale Fénix del lugar y se da cuenta de que hay un grupo de amigos bastante grande, celebrando una despedida de soltero. Como no es un evento programado, no está la coordinación que debería, así que bailan, beben y ríen por todos lados.

Capítulo 10: Triple show

Suena por parlantes: "Estrella, Ámbar y Cleo a camarines". Fénix les indica que se cambien de ropa para un baile triple, y así encender la despedida que allí se está celebrando. Se escucha nuevamente en parlantes: "Tomen asiento, se viene el gran show de la noche. ¿Dónde está el novio? Que levante la mano. ¡Querido público de Nocturnas! Para celebrar la despedida de soltero de este hombre, les presentaremos un baile o show triple con las más sensuales y osadas chicas de Nocturnas. Así que los invito a tomar asiento porque el show está a punto de empezar".

Mientras se cambian de ropa, las chicas conversan sobre el ambiente en el local y cómo harán el baile triple. Hay veces en que llevan gran ensayo, pero en otras es más del cincuenta por ciento improvisación. Las chicas se conocen, por lo tanto, no les cuesta mucho trabajo complementarse en la pista.

—Amiga, ¿y si nos tomamos algo para los nervios?

—Ya, sí estaría bueno. Ámbar, pídela tú ahora.

—Ok, yo no he pedido mi colación aún, así que la comparto para bajar el nerviosismo.

—Pídelo bien cargado, eso sí —insiste Estrella.

—Ok.

A pesar de trabajar en un lugar donde te pagan por beber y mientras más copas te paguen, más dinero ganas, las chicas no acostumbran a tomar demasiado alcohol, ya que son las encargadas de pagar todo lo que el cliente compra. Por ende, están bien controladas con respecto al consumo de alcohol. Es por eso que la copa que beben muchas veces es jugo, agua o alguna gaseosa. A esta última, en ocasiones, le ponen un poco de alcohol para entrar en confianza, dicen. También se les permite tomar un vaso de algún trago con alcohol que quieran, una "colación", como le llaman en el club.

—Ya, yo estoy lista —dice Cleo.

—Yo igual.

—A mí me falta la capa para salir y listo.

—Ya, estamos listas para salir. —le avisan a Rubén, el encargado de la música y de coordinar todos los bailes, quien avisa por parlantes que el show comienza para que todos se acomoden y tomen su lugar.

Suena "Earned it", de The Weeknd. Las chicas, una a una, van saliendo a la pista, con una caminata sensual al ritmo de la música. Las tres lucen una capa negra y en sus rostros, un antifaz. Se mueven alrededor del caño, caminan y giran en sí mismas, dejando ver en cada vuelta lo osado y sensual de su atuendo. Se acercan levemente a los clientes y vuelven a tomar el caño con mucha coordinación, obligando a todos a su alrededor a estar muy concentrados en sus movimientos.

Estrella toma de la mano al novio y lo trae a la pista, lo posiciona en el caño con las manos hacia arriba, mientras las tres giran en torno a él, como los planetas alrededor del sol. Le susurran en el oído, pasan sus manos por su cuerpo, las frotan desde su pelo hasta su cintura. A la vez, se quitan las capas con mucha sensualidad. A pesar de los gritos, aplausos y alboroto dentro del local por el show, las chicas siguen concentradas en sus movimientos, interactuando con otros asistentes mientras se van despojando de sus apretadas y sensuales prendas, quedando solo en ropa interior. Van acomodando a los clientes en sus asientos ya que la canción está a punto de terminar. Se reagrupan en el caño cuando comienza la próxima canción, "Mala Santa", de Becky G.

Se mueven de arriba abajo en el caño dándose la espalda una contra otra, teniendo cubierto así todo su alrededor. Justo en el segundo 30 de la canción, uno de los asistentes se levanta con la intención de ir al baño, pero Estrella le pone una mano en el pecho y lo lleva de vuelta a su sitio, al mismo tiempo que las otras chicas se dirigen directo a los clientes, ahora con una actitud de empoderamiento y decididas, con movimientos eróticos y mostrando quienes son las que mandan en el local. Se suben en las piernas de los clientes, uno por uno los hacen participar a todos, tomándolos por sorpresa. Esta vez, los clientes quedan perplejos observando, algunos esperando que alguna de las chicas se les acerque, otros, queriendo pasar desapercibidos. Atónitos con la segunda parte del show, no se dan cuenta de cuán rápido pasó esa canción y termina. Ovación para las tres bailarinas.

Capítulo 11: Final

Terminado el show, las chicas se apresuran en el cambio de vestuario para volver rápidamente con los clientes y sacar provecho al baile que hicieron, ya que todos están entusiasmados, querrán compartir con ellas. Cerca de las cuatro de la madrugada, la jornada laboral en el café Nocturnas está llegando a su fin y las chicas lo sienten. A esta hora, las piernas les pesan por los bailes, tienen los pies hinchados por la extensa jornada con zapatos de tacón. Algunas, a esta altura, sienten dolor de cabeza, producto de la fuerte música, combinado con la gran paciencia que se tiene con algunos clientes. Después de avisar al público que quedan pocos minutos para el cierre, todos se apresuran para comprar su último trago. Algunos pagan a las chicas los últimos bailes privados, y otros, para quienes se va a acabar la noche, encuentran el valor para hablar con más confianza e invitar a las chicas a seguir la fiesta en otro lugar. Unos pocos intentan conseguir algún número para lograr concretar en otro lugar lo que en el local no pudieron, y algunos también, los menos, se van enamorados.

Con Nocturnas sin clientes, se encienden las luces. En menos de cinco minutos pasa de la música fuerte y el alboroto a la tranquilidad y el silencio. Mientras las chicas se cambian de ropa y se quitan el maquillaje, el encargado cuadra la caja para finalizar las ventas y pagos del día. La luz blanca ilumina cada rincón, dejando ver muchas cosas que en la oscuridad no se veían: los vasos que se dieron vuelta, algún vidrio en las esquinas, las manchas en el piso, un juego de llaves olvidado en el sillón. Aun en el silencio y vacío del café, se logra visualizar el caos que en un momento se vivió, y una jornada más se acaba. Luego vendrá otra, no se sabe cómo, si será mañana, quién asistirá, cómo estará, mucho menos qué pasará, pero sea como sea, para sus clientes, lo que viven en Café Nocturnas, en Nocturnas se queda...

FIN

Agradecimientos

Este libro está inspirado en los prejuicios, la ilusión, la verdad, la mentira y, sobre todo, en la valentía de las mujeres que hacen cualquier cosa por su familia. Está dedicado a todas las mujeres de la noche, a aquellas chicas que soportan ser llamadas sucias, a las damas de la vida fácil, que si fuera tan fácil, lo haría cualquiera.

Ellas me demostraron que muchas veces una esposa cualquiera es mucho más objeto que ellas mismas; son las que utilizan a los hombres para su beneficio. Aquí, ellas controlan, ellas mandan, ellas deciden; son las reinas de la noche.

Muchas gracias a todas las chicas nocturnas que compartieron sus experiencias conmigo. Gracias por dejarme entrar en su mundo, con sus penas y alegrías. Gracias por permitirme mostrar al mundo parte de esa vida que su entorno y cercanos no conocen. Y, por supuesto, sus identidades conmigo siempre estarán a salvo.